The Last Loon

ORCA
YOUNG
READERS

The Last Loon

REBECCA UPJOHN

ORCA BOOK PUBLISHERS

Library and Archives Canada Cataloguing in Publication

Upjohn, Rebecca, 1962-
The last loon / written by Rebecca Upjohn Snyder.
(Orca young readers)

Issued also in an electronic format.
ISBN 978-1-55469-292-7

I. Title. II. Series: Orca young readers
PS8641.P386L38 2010   jC813'.6   C2010-903532-1

First published in the United States, 2010
Library of Congress Control Number: 2010928829

Summary: When city-boy Evan realizes that a loon is about to die in the middle of a fast-freezing lake near his aunt's cottage, he decides to rescue it, risking his own life in the process.

Mixed Sources
Product group from well-managed forests,
controlled sources and recycled wood or fiber
www.fsc.org Cert no. SW-COC-000952
© 1996 Forest Stewardship Council

Orca Book Publishers is dedicated to preserving the environment and has printed this book on paper certified by the Forest Stewardship Council.

Orca Book Publishers gratefully acknowledges the support for its publishing programs provided by the following agencies: the Government of Canada through the Canada Book Fund and the Canada Council for the Arts, and the Province of British Columbia through the BC Arts Council and the Book Publishing Tax Credit.

Typesetting by Nadja Penaluna
Cover artwork by Ken Dewar
Author photo by Kendall Townend

ORCA BOOK PUBLISHERS
PO Box 5626, Stn. B
Victoria, BC Canada
V8R 6S4

ORCA BOOK PUBLISHERS
PO Box 468
Custer, WA USA
98240-0468

www.orcabook.com
Printed and bound in Canada.
13 12 11 10 • 4 3 2 1

For Mum and Dad

Contents

CHAPTER 1

Alone in the Wilderness

The sound of Mom's car faded into the freezing wind as she drove away. I still couldn't believe she'd left me here. A zillion miles from anywhere. Alone.

I wanted to stand on the dirt track until Dad picked me up again. But Dad was in the Northwest Territories at the diamond mine. He wouldn't be back until his two-week shift was over.

"Come on in, Evan," said Aunt Mag. "You must be hungry after your trip. Boys are always hungry." She strode away. I didn't have any choice. I followed.

Okay, so I wasn't exactly alone. I was with my aunt. But I barely knew her. And she had a shady past. She'd been in jail. I was sure that's why she lived so far from civilization. Dad said she was a bit loony.

I guess he can say that because he's her brother. When I said it to Mom, though, she got mad.

"Evan," Mom said, "just because someone marches to their own drummer, doesn't mean there is anything wrong with them." Then she said that being up here with Aunt Mag would be good for me. Whenever she says stuff like that, I know I won't be having any fun.

Mom could have taken me with her to England. She just didn't want to. She'd said she couldn't look after me and Granny at the same time. Especially after my recent behavior. I asked her why Granny couldn't stay in the hospital and rest her hip until after Christmas. Mom got all squinchy around the eyes, the way she does when she's really steamed.

"You're eleven years old, for goodness sake," she'd said. "It's time you thought of someone other than yourself, Evan Kemp!" When she adds my last name, I know I'm in trouble. And so here I was at Aunt Mag's for the whole Christmas break.

My aunt disappeared into her house. I paused and looked around. I'd only been here once before, when I was really little, so I didn't remember much. The house was small, more like a cottage, with light brown sides and a red metal roof. It stood in a clearing surrounded by a forest of giant trees. Not too far from the house, six big blue panels tilted to the sky. I got a bad feeling in my stomach looking at them. Was she trying to communicate with aliens? What if she *was* an alien?

There was also a tall pole with a little propeller on the top whirling in the wind. A windmill? What the heck was that for? I remembered Dad saying that Aunt Mag lived off the grid. It had something to do with how you got your electricity, but I wasn't paying too much attention at the time. Now I wish I had.

A Canadian flag flapped on a flagpole by the door. At least that was normal. The trees at the edge of the clearing shook their shaggy selves, and something in the forest creaked. I shivered. The forest was dark and eerie, perfect for an ex-con avoiding the eyes of the law. I heard a whooshing noise beyond the house. I could see water through the trees. I had forgotten that Aunt Mag lived on a lake. I hated lakes. The water was always cold, and creepy things lived there. Things that wriggled and squished and brushed up against you when you went swimming. Not that I planned to have anything to do with this lake anyway. It was way too cold for swimming. I shuddered and ran for the house.

CHAPTER 2

Respect

I shoved open the door and walked into a small room with a tile floor. On my left was the glass wall of a sunroom crammed with plants. It looked like a jungle. I guess my aunt didn't have enough forest outside. She needed it inside too. A couple of raggedy coats and a parka with duct-tape patches hung on hooks on the other wall. Gloves and mitts lay on a bench made from branches. Lined up under the coats were boots and shoes. It was all disgustingly tidy. I hung my jacket next to the parka and shoved my boots in with the other ones. I found Aunt Mag in the kitchen, peering at the lake through an enormous pair of binoculars. She didn't notice me.

"Aunt Mag?" I said.

She jumped. "Crikey, Evan! Don't sneak up on me like that. You'll give me a heart attack." She waved me over to the table.

I went and sat down. "What were you looking at?"

She looked back out the big window. "There's a loon out there. It's been hanging around the last few weeks. Usually they've all migrated by now, but the weather has been so warm this fall." She shook her head and frowned. "I'm a bit worried that the lake will freeze over suddenly and the loon won't have enough open water to take off." She offered me the binoculars.

"A loon?" I said.

"You know. The bird on the one-dollar coin? That's why it's called a loonie."

Duh! Everyone knew that. But why was she so interested? I took a look. Everything was blurry. I felt Aunt Mag's hands helping me adjust the focus. A black bird with a white band around its neck and a pattern of white spots on its back jumped into view. Its head turned and I could see it better. It had a white chest, a long sharp bill and…"Whoa! Red eyes?" I lowered the binoculars and stared at my aunt.

Aunt Mag grinned at my surprise. "Some researchers think the red eyes may be a type of camouflage for loons underwater."

"To hide from lake monsters?"

She laughed. "More so they can sneak up on their food."

"Oh," I said.

"Also," said Aunt Mag, "only adult loons have red eyes and usually only in breeding season, so we think it may be something to do with breeding too. We don't really know for sure. It's kind of exciting."

I glued my eyes back to the binoculars and watched the bird bob on the waves. Then it dipped headfirst into the water and slipped out of sight. I watched and waited, but there was no sign of it. "Where is it?"

"It's probably diving for food," Aunt Mag said. "It can stay under for a minute or so, and it may come up quite far from where it dove. Loons are master swimmers. And they can be pretty tricky if they don't want to be seen."

I scanned the water. Nothing.

Maybe this one had learned how to turn invisible. That's what you get in the wilderness. You think you're going to see moose and beavers and stuff, but all you get are bug bites and boredom. Grown-ups get excited if they find animal poop. Proof that there is wildlife around, my dad says, even if you can't see it. I didn't need the wilderness to see animal poop. There is plenty of it in the park near my house. Same with birds. I could see them any day at home. I put down the binoculars.

"Wish I knew why it was hanging around," Aunt Mag muttered. Then she looked at me. "I'm forgetting myself. You must be starved. I made some soup."

She brought two steaming bowls to the table.

I looked down and swallowed hard. It was full of mystery stuff, all mooshed together. No way I was eating that.

Aunt Mag frowned. "What's the trouble?"

"I don't like this kind of soup," I said. Then I remembered Mom telling me a million times to be polite at Aunt Mag's, so I added, "Thank you."

Aunt Mag's eyebrows snapped down. "How on earth do you know? You haven't tasted it."

"I know," I explained. "I can tell."

"I see," she said. She nodded and then shrugged. "Okay." She took my bowl to the counter and came back to the table. She continued eating.

I couldn't believe it. Was she going to starve me? "Mom usually gives me pizza or pasta if there's something I don't like," I said.

"Your mom isn't here," said Aunt Mag.

That did it. Forget being polite. I jumped up. "No, she isn't, but that isn't my fault! I didn't ask to come here. I didn't want to. But since my parents decided to abandon me, I'm stuck here. If you make me eat your soup, I'll barf. Is that what you want?" I ran to the mudroom, grabbed my jacket and bolted outside.

"Evan—" I heard Aunt Mag call. I slammed the door with all my might. The whole house shook. I ran down the steps and along a stone path to the sandy beach, where I yelled at the sky. I snatched up some rocks by the shore and heaved one after the other into the water, throwing and throwing until my arm hurt.

I found an old wooden chair on the beach and flopped down into it. The wind slapped spray into the air. The waves couldn't make up their minds which way to go. I felt the cold air poking its nasty fingers through my jacket. But I couldn't go back inside.

Aunt Mag arrived and sat down on the ground next to me. "This is a good spot to think," she said.

I didn't answer.

She turned a little to face me. "Look, Evan. Your mom and dad didn't abandon you. Your grandmother didn't mean to break her hip. And your dad is new at the mine so he's got the shift no one else wants. Your folks just figured that you'd have more fun and be happier up here than if you stayed in the city with a new sitter." She stopped.

I knew what she wasn't saying. I had heard Mom talking to her on the phone. "I don't know what to do with him, Mag. He keeps getting sent home from school. He isn't a bad kid, he's just…well, he has a lot of energy. He gets bored and that's when he gets into trouble." And that's why Mom wouldn't take me to England. I don't mean to get into trouble. I only went on the school roof because the caretaker wouldn't get the ball down. It wasn't really dangerous. Unfortunately the principal didn't agree. And Mom didn't agree. And even though Dad laughed about it, he said I had to show some respect.

Respect. As if they respected what I wanted.

Aunt Mag sighed. "I know you didn't want to come here."

Yeah, she had that right. I stared out at the lake.

"We're having a bonfire on the beach tomorrow night," she said. "The neighbors are coming. They have a boy about your age, named Cedar. Once you meet some other kids, I'm sure things will be better."

A bonfire sounded pretty cool, but I wasn't about to admit it to Aunt Mag.

She waited for a moment; then she stood up. "Come on up when you're ready."

I sat there until she disappeared. I was about to follow her when the loony bird popped up in the cove. It glided back and forth as if it was looking at me. Then it came closer. It was bigger than I first thought, way bigger. It slipped through the water, checking me out. It was close enough that I could really see its weird red eyes. Cool and creepy at the same time.

"Hello, bird," I called.

It turned and dove. I waited for it to come back up, but it didn't. I scanned the whole lake, but it never showed. Great. Abandoned by a bird too.

CHAPTER 3

Hairy Tarantulas

Aunt Mag must have felt a little sorry for me because, when I got back to the house, she had made me a cheese sandwich and some hot chocolate. She never mentioned the soup. I showed her some respect and thanked her.

As I was eating, I looked around. The kitchen had yellow walls and a wood ceiling. One of the small rooms leading off the kitchen was blue. Another was green. I liked how they went together. The window and door openings were fat and curved, not straight and flat like in a regular house.

Aunt Mag caught me checking things out. "This is a straw-bale house," she said. "In case you're wondering."

"A what?" I said.

"The walls are made of straw with plaster over top."

I chuckled. "You're kidding, right?"

She shook her head. "No, come and see."

I followed her into the living room next to the kitchen. She led me over to a little diamond-shaped window in the wall. Instead of a view outside, it looked inside the wall. I saw a tuft of yellow hay. "This is called a 'truth window,'" she said as she unlatched it. "Go ahead. Feel the straw."

I did. It was the real thing. I looked at my aunt. Her mouth twitched. What else did she have up her sleeve?

"And notice how warm your feet are?" she went on.

I wriggled my toes in my socks and nodded.

"There are tubes running underneath the floor. They're filled with water heated by the sun."

Yeah, right. "How does the sun get into water under the floor?" I asked.

"The blue solar panels outside catch energy from the sun. Whatever energy doesn't get used right away gets stored in huge batteries. And the wind-mill generates some power too. They give me heat and electricity."

"Oh," I said. "I thought those panels were for…"
I stopped in a hurry.

A smile spread over Aunt Mag's face. "For what? Sending messages to Mars?"

I felt my face turn red.

She let out a big laugh when she saw my reaction.

I shrugged as if I didn't care. "So, why do you live in a straw house?"

"Straw is easy to grow. All the materials in this house are either from local sources or are easily renewable. And they don't poison the Earth." She smiled and patted the wall as if it was her pet. "Also, I helped build it." When she realized I was staring at her, she dropped her hand and shoved it in her pocket. "And it doesn't cost as much to run because it uses energy in a smart way. All my power comes from the sun and the wind. I have a generator for backup but I very rarely have to use it. Most of the time I end up lending it out to other people when *their* power gets knocked out."

I nodded. That *was* smart. "Okay, but straw?" I pointed at the fire flickering in the black metal stove near the wall. "Aren't you afraid it'll burn down?"

"Nope," said Aunt Mag. "The folks who design these houses know how to make them safe."

I examined my aunt a little more carefully. Maybe she did know a thing or two after all. Her house was a bit strange, but it was comfortable and it was definitely cosy.

"Cool," I said, because it really was.

After I finished my snack, Aunt Mag showed me where I was going to be sleeping. She heaved my suitcase up a wood ladder to a narrow walkway outside a loft. It was above the jungle room.

"It's the snuggest spot in the house," she said. She shoved the door open with a grunt.

"I meant to fix that," she muttered. She plopped my bag down and I walked in. The roof sloped on either side, but there were big windows and it was really bright and warm. It felt like a tree house. Maybe I would ask for a loft bedroom when I got home.

"Make yourself at home, Evan," said Aunt Mag. "I'll be down below if you need anything."

I dumped my knapsack on the floor and plunked myself onto the bed. A cloud of dust puffed up in the air, making me sneeze. I lay back on the pillows, ready to relax. I gazed up. I hate to admit it, but I screamed.

A hairy spider the size of a hockey puck squatted in a web in the corner of the window above my head. It waggled its front feet and then scrunched down, getting ready to leap on my face. I crossed the room and flew out the door in one amazing leap. I nearly knocked my aunt off the top of the ladder.

"Evan, what's the matter?" Her face was white and her eyes bulged.

I tried to keep my teeth from clacking together as I pointed into the room. I finally managed to stutter out, "S-s-spider!"

My aunt's mouth dropped open as she looked at me and then into the room. Understanding suddenly reached her brain. "You screamed because of a spider?"

I nodded.

She sank to the floor. "Evan, I thought you'd hurt yourself or something." She let her breath out in a whoosh.

"It's ginormous!" I said. "It was getting ready to attack and sink its poisonous fangs into my face! It's a tarantula or something."

Aunt Mag hooted. "Evan, we don't have tarantulas here. And most spiders are more afraid of you than you are of them."

I doubted that. I'm not afraid of much, but I *hate* spiders.

Aunt Mag obviously didn't though. She went into my room and caught the spider in an old mug sitting on the dresser. "Come on, my friend," she said. She tucked its hairy legs in and covered it with her hand. "You're safe now." Somehow I don't think she meant me.

"I'm not sleeping in there," I said. "There might be a whole hive of babies hiding somewhere, waiting for dark."

My aunt let out a great big snort. "Spiders don't live in hives," she said, but she straightened her face pretty quickly when she realized I didn't think any of this was funny. "Okay," she said. "Let me take care of this"—she held up the mug—"and then we can clean your loft. I should have done it before you got here, but I ran out of time."

I waited on the walkway for her. Aunt Mag did the cleaning while I supervised. I was right about babies hiding in wait. She found six smaller versions of the tarantula and about two hundred dead flies. Little dried-up corpses lying with their legs in the air. That's another problem with the wilderness. When wildlife does show up, it acts like it owns the place.

Finally the room was debugged and Aunt Mag went downstairs while I unpacked. Once I had hung my Maple Leafs poster on the slope above the bed, I felt better. I looked out the window. There was a blob in the middle of the lake. It was hard to see in the fading light, but I knew what it was. That bird again. Why would anything hang around out there all alone, especially at this time of year? I guess that's why it was called a loon.

CHAPTER 4

Ex-Con

The next morning as I munched on my toast, the kitchen door burst open. Aunt Mag nearly choked on her tea. Someone bundled up in outdoor clothes barged in and shouted, "We'regonnagetourtree.CanEvancome?"

"I beg your pardon?" said Aunt Mag after she stopped coughing.

The person pulled off his scarf and hat. A boy about my age said, "We're gonna get our tree. Can Evan come?"

"Oh," said Aunt Mag. "Sure, if he wants." She turned to me for an answer.

I didn't have a clue what they were talking about, but the boy's grin was so huge that I found myself grinning back.

"I'm Cedar," he said. "We're going to cut a Christmas tree. Want to come?"

I nodded as I gulped down the last of my toast. Then I rushed to the mudroom, grabbed my coat and hauled on my boots. I followed Cedar out the door to where his dad, Mac, was waiting in a humungous truck. Cedar's two younger sisters sat in the backseat.

"We always bring Kait and Trinnie," whispered Cedar. "Dad says girls can be foresters just as much as boys."

I rolled my eyes.

Cedar leaned closer. "You're lucky you don't have sisters."

I snickered. "My best friend Henry has three."

"Gross," said Cedar. He made a barfing sound. It was awesome. I was definitely going to practice.

We turned off the main road and bounced along a track that went deeper into the woods. We stopped in an open area where huge tree trunks lay piled higher than our heads. We slid out of the cab. I took a deep breath. The air smelled like Christmas trees.

"Grab the tools, and let's find a tree," Mac said. He walked off past the log pile, carrying an ax almost as big as me. The girls each took some clippers and scampered off after their dad. Cedar grabbed a saw with dangerous-looking teeth. I really wanted one too, but I didn't see another one.

"There's a hatchet," Cedar said. "You can bring that."

A bunch of tools lay there, but which one was a hatchet? I didn't know this country stuff. Why would I? Cedar hopped around, impatient to get going, so I said, "Naw, it's okay. I'll just watch."

Cedar stopped hopping and frowned at me.

"Shouldn't we go?" I said. "If I was you, I wouldn't want to miss the chance to use that saw."

"I'll get the hatchet," he said. He pulled out a mini-ax and held it up next to his saw. "You can have whichever ya want."

"Hey, thanks!" I never got to use tools like this at home. Mom didn't believe in letting me in the same room with sharp objects. She was still steamed about the time I helped redecorate the living room by chiseling a zigzag design in the new mantle over the fireplace. And guess who gave me the toolkit to develop my creativity in the first place? Mom, that's who. I chose the hatchet and we headed off.

"So, we're really going to cut down a tree?" I asked.

"Yep," said Cedar.

"Sweet," I said. Then I remembered about how chopping down trees was bad. "But isn't that bad for the environment or something? Don't we need the trees to keep on breathing?"

"You sound like your Aunt Mag," Cedar said.

"No, I don't!" How could he think that? I almost handed the hatchet back.

Cedar snickered. "Only with her it's animals."

"What?" I said. "What do you mean?"

"Don't get her going about animal rights," Cedar advised. "She gets all red in the face and starts shouting." He laughed. "Once she threw a plate at my dad. He was stirring her up just to make her mad, and boy, did she get mad! That was before she went to jail, of course. She did anger management after that, so now she just takes deep breaths and stomps outside."

I stopped walking. I had completely forgotten that my aunt had spent time behind bars. I couldn't believe it. How could I forget? I grabbed Cedar's arm. I had to know the truth. "Why did Aunt Mag go to jail?"

"Don't you know?" he said.

I shook my head.

"Smuggling," said Cedar.

"*What*? Aunt Mag is a smuggler?" I couldn't believe my ears.

"No, not her. She caught a guy smuggling turtles."

"*Turtles*?" This was getting weirder by the second.

"Not because she caught him though," said Cedar. He snickered. "Because she *punched* him."

Oh great! I was living with a *violent* ex-con.

"My dad will tell you the whole thing."

While Cedar and his sisters attempted to cut down a pine tree, Mac told me about my aunt's trip to jail.

"Mag was doing research on the Spotted Turtle. She noticed the numbers were declining where she was conducting her study, so she set up a field camp for a few weeks to watch. She saw a man trapping them. She pretended she wanted to buy one and found out that he was smuggling the turtles out of the country. He was selling them illegally as exotic pets. There is a big demand for turtles on the black market. Spotted Turtles are protected. They were already at risk because their habitat was disappearing and there were fewer and fewer of them anyway. This just made her crazy." He paused and helped Trinnie unstick her clippers from a tree branch.

"Mag confronted the smuggler and threatened him. But she didn't have enough proof to go to the police. *He* called the police and complained about her, and they warned her not to harass him. She got the Ministry of Natural Resources to send a conservation officer to keep an eye out for the guy, but after a few days of seeing nothing, the officer went away. Mag didn't believe that the smuggler had given up. One turtle could fetch several hundred dollars. It was easy money for him. So she waited, watched and took photos. She found two local witnesses who had seen the same man setting traps and collecting turtles. They agreed to write accounts of what they'd seen. Eventually she had enough evidence to take to the police. They charged him, but he hired a high-powered lawyer who got him off the charges.

"Mag was in a crowd of protesters outside the courthouse. When the smuggler walked past her, he smirked at her. Mag lost it. She socked him. Broke his nose and gave him a beauty of a shiner." Mac grinned. "She spent two nights in jail before the guy dropped the assault charges." His grin got wider. "It was the photo of Mag punching him out that did it. After that picture came out in every newspaper, people jumped on the cause of saving the Spotted Turtle. The smuggler vanished." He laughed and shook his head. "Just don't mention turtle smuggling around your aunt unless you need some lively entertainment."

I imagined my aunt breaking someone's nose to save a turtle. She was crazy enough to do it. And if she was that way about turtles, maybe it explained hairy tarantulas and loony birds too.

The tree Cedar and his sisters had been cutting sagged to one side. "Hey, Evan, we need your hatchet," Cedar called.

I rushed over. Cedar and the girls stood back. they It was obvious they expected me to chop the thing down using my mad hatchet skills. How hard could it be? I raised the hatchet overhead and swung down with a mighty force. *Thwap.* The blade missed the place they'd been cutting and the hatchet bounced off the tree. My face got hot. Obviously it was harder than I thought.

"You gotta hit the same spot," Cedar said helpfully.

"Here," said Mac. "Let me show you."

Trinnie pulled me way back. Mac made a quick chop. The tree dropped to the ground. I looked at his ax and then at mine.

Mac saw me and chuckled. "Takes practice," he said. "Once you get past the bouncing stage, it gets a little more rewarding." They were all laughing now. How was I supposed to know how to chop a tree? I'd never done it before. Mac took the hatchet from my hands and felt the blade. "'Course, it would have been better if Cedar had given you the one that had been sharpened first. This wouldn't even cut through snow." He squeezed my shoulder. "Don't feel bad, Evan. The first time I tried using a hatchet, not only did it bounce off the wood, it hit me in the forehead on the rebound."

I doubted it was true, but it made me feel a whole lot better.

CHAPTER 5

Girl Jobs

Cedar had to babysit and Aunt Mag was muttering over her computer, so I hung around in my loft most of the afternoon using my pocket game player. I kept looking out the window. I wanted it to get dark so we could have the bonfire. Finally I heard a rumbly voice talking to Aunt Mag, and I went down to investigate.

"Oh, Evan, good. This is Peter Spencer, my colleague," Aunt Mag said. "He's also Cedar's uncle."

"Glad to meet you at long last, Evan. Call me Peter." His smile was just as friendly as Cedar's and Mac's.

"Peter brought pizza from town," said Aunt Mag. "We thought you might like that."

I looked at her, surprised. Maybe she understood kids better than I thought. Then she said something to me that made me sure she didn't.

"Would you please set the table for the three of us?"

I stared at her. I never did that kind of stuff at home. I mean, the kitchen was pretty much Mom's territory. Girls did that kind of thing. "Isn't that your job?" I said.

Aunt Mag's face turned red. A little too late, I remembered her history of violence.

"Whooo, boy," said Peter quietly.

"What did you say?" my aunt asked. Her voice sounded funny, sort of choked off.

"What he said," said Peter, grabbing my arm, "was 'Where are the plates?'" He dragged me over to the counter, opened a cupboard and pointed at a stack of them.

I didn't really want to turn my back on my aunt, but Peter gave me a nudge. I reached up and pulled out three plates. I could feel Aunt Mag's laser-beam eyes in the back of my head. What was her problem anyway? I was thinking of asking, when Peter slid open a drawer with cutlery in it. I didn't really see why we needed any for eating pizza, but he twitched his head toward them. It was clear that I was supposed to take some. I pulled out a few knives and forks and plunked them on top of the plates. Peter jerked his thumb at the table. I took the whole pile over. Then I got glasses and napkins.

"Well," said Peter, rubbing his hands together. "I'm starved." He pulled a large pizza box out of the oven and flashed a smile at my aunt. She was still giving me the evil eye. Her lips were pinched shut and her breath whistled through her nose. The phone rang. Aunt Mag marched away to answer it.

Peter served three huge slices of pizza onto my plate. "'Round here, jobs have no gender attached to them. Best to remember that," he said. I must have looked as confused as I felt because he tried to explain things again. "Everyone does every job here. There are no 'boy jobs' or 'girl jobs.' It may not be what you're used to, but you'd better learn fast."

"But my mom does all this kitchen stuff," I said.

"Frankly, I can't believe your mom lets you and your dad get away with that," he said.

"Well, Dad helps sometimes," I said. "Like if Mom's working late or something, but it's really her job."

Peter shook his head like he couldn't believe what he was hearing. "What's your job?" he asked.

"Job?" I said. "I'm a kid. I don't do jobs."

"Well, now you do. Setting the table is one. Doing dishes is another. We'll start with those two. I'll show you how; then you can work your way back into your aunt's good books."

I hated it when grown-ups ganged up on kids. It was so not fair. I thought about not eating, just to get even, but the smell of pizza was killing me. I decided this was not the time to argue. I'd figure it out later. I took a big bite and didn't stop until I'd scarfed down all three pieces.

Aunt Mag came back to the table. "That was Cedar on the phone," she said. "They'll be along soon."

Peter nodded.

Aunt Mag narrowed her eyes at me. "There'll be just enough time to do the dishes."

"Evan and I'll do them, Mag," said Peter before I could say anything.

"But—," I protested.

"Good books, remember?" Peter said out of the corner of his mouth. His eyes flicked significantly toward Aunt Mag who was cutting up a piece of pizza on her plate.

"But why do we have to do them now?" I asked.

Peter grimaced just as Aunt Mag looked up. Her eyebrows snapped down. "What's going on?" she demanded.

"Nothing!" Peter's smile sparkled at her. "Relax and eat, Mag. Take your time."

Aunt Mag ate her pizza and glared at me, so I kept quiet. We sat in silence. After a couple of minutes Peter checked his watch. Another minute later his left knee started to jiggle up and down under the table. Aunt Mag reached for another slice. Peter slid the box closer to her. She frowned. Peter shifted in his chair. Aunt Mag went back to eating. She must have heard that rule that you're supposed to chew each mouthful thirty-two times before you swallow. Both of Peter's knees jiggled now and mine felt twitchy.

A moment later Peter jumped up from the table. "I think we'll just get started. Come on, Evan. It'll only take a couple of minutes."

I followed Peter to the sink.

Peter washed the dishes while I watched.

"Why doesn't Aunt Mag have a dishwasher?" I grumbled.

"Waste of water and power," said Peter. He handed me a plate dribbling water and soapsuds. "Go ahead and dry it."

I took it and swiped the dishcloth over the front. The cloth soaked up most of the water and burst the bubbles, so I put the plate in the cupboard. The dish-towel was sopping already.

"It's best to dry the back too," he said as he handed me a second plate. "That way when you take them out again they aren't covered in mold."

"Eww!" I rubbed a bit more carefully and managed to spread the wetness evenly back and front this time.

As Aunt Mag took her final bite, Peter whisked her plate off the table and passed it through the bubbles. He put it in the dish rack. Then he grabbed the cutlery in one bundle and swooshed it through the soapy water and dropped it, *crash*, into the rack.

"I'm not sure you're the best person to teach Evan dishwashing techniques," Aunt Mag said.

"We're done," said Peter. He snatched my dish-towel away before I could finish the last plate and whipped it onto an overhead drying rack. He tugged it straight. "That's the goal, isn't it?" He waggled his eyebrows at her.

My aunt let out a snort of disapproval but her mouth twitched. She looked at me. "Evan, bundle up carefully: snow pants, scarf, extra socks. The temperature is dropping fast."

I stared at her in disgust. I wasn't exactly two. I know you have to wear extra stuff when it's cold out.

She ignored my look. "If you need long johns, I have extras in the bottom drawer of my dresser. Help yourself." I was speechless. She didn't seem to notice my shock. She strode out of the room.

I heard a muffled laugh behind me and spun around. But Peter stood with his hands behind his back and stared out the window as if the offer of old lady underwear was normal conversation around here.

CHAPTER 6

Bonfire

Aunt Mag came back carrying some flashlights. "All right. Let's go down and light the fire. Evan, could you please bring that pile of blankets?"

I avoided looking at Peter as I put on my outdoor gear. I stepped out under the porch light, and the cold sucked my breath away. My aunt sure wasn't kidding about the temperature drop.

"Margaret!" Mac climbed out of his enormous truck. "Did you plan this for the coldest night of the year on purpose?"

"Year's not over, Mac," she called back.

He threw back his head and laughed.

Kait and Trinnie chased each other around the truck, flitting in and out of the light like moths. Cedar charged over to me. "I just found out our rink will be ready maybe tomorrow and we'll be able to play shinny."

"You have a rink?" I asked.

Cedar shrugged. "Yeah, we make one every winter. I heard you were good at hockey. Did you bring your skates?"

"No. I didn't know I'd need them." Why hadn't Mom packed them? She had probably forgotten that her only child might want to have a little fun while she was away.

"No problem," said Cedar. "We'll find you some. What are you doing holding those for?" He nodded at the blankets in my arms.

"My aunt told me to carry them down to the beach."

Cedar scowled. "Let's get out of here before they get us to do any more crummy jobs!"

"Make yourself useful, Cedar." Mac strode by with an enormous basket. "There's more to bring from the truck." He paused and winked at me. "Hello, Evan. Good to see one of you is working."

"I'm helping Evan," Cedar protested.

"How, exactly?" asked a lady who I figured must be Cedar's mom. She smiled at me. "Hello, Evan. I'm Pat."

"Hi," I said.

Kait and Trinnie raced past, nearly knocking us down. Cedar yelled at them. They just kept going. He grabbed half the blankets.

I followed him through the trees and down the path.

Cedar and I got to light the fire. Everyone sat down on the logs around it. I felt toasty with the flames on my face and a blanket around my back. After a bit, Pat unloaded the basket. She passed around Clementine oranges, moose-shaped sugar cookies and homemade pretzels. Then she offered us wieners to roast. She set out ketchup, mustard, relish and sauerkraut on a board raised on two cement blocks.

"I have some veggie dogs too, if you'd prefer, Evan." Pat smiled at me.

Mac speared two wieners on a long fork and held them over the flames. They smelled so good. I wished I hadn't eaten so much pizza.

"Want a s'more?" Cedar asked. He handed me a box of graham crackers.

"A what?" I looked inside the package.

"You don't know what a s'more is?" Kait asked. She made it sound as though I was the last person on earth who didn't know.

"I'll make you one," offered Trinnie.

"Trinnie makes good ones," said Cedar.

"I make better ones!" protested Kait.

"No, you don't," said Cedar. "Trinnie's are better."

"You're a poo-poo head!" Kait shouted.

"That's enough, Kaitlyn," said Mac.

After a few minutes, Trinnie handed me an oozing blob of melted chocolate and scorched marshmallow squished between two graham crackers.

"It's better than it looks," Cedar said in my ear.

I took a bite. To my surprise it *was* good. I took another huge mouthful.

"Want more?" Trinnie asked.

"I'd go slow, if I were you," Pat warned. "One bite too many and they tend to come back up again."

I nearly choked as everyone else laughed.

"I'll take one, Trinnie," Mag said.

Trinnie made them for everyone.

"How about a song?" Pat said.

"Ninety-nine bottles of beer on the wall!" Cedar shouted.

He was drowned out by all the grown-ups yelling, "NO!"

"I've got one," said Mac. He started singing. "My eyes are dim, I cannot see. I have not brought my specs with me. I haaave no-ot brought my-y specs…with…me."

Peter took over. "There was Kait, Kait, with a stomach ache, in the store…in the store…"

Kait's mouth was full of s'more so all she could do was squeak. Mac and Cedar sang with Peter. "There was Kait, Kait, with a stomach ache in the corner grocery sto-o-ore. My eyes are dim, I cannot see. I have not brought my specs with me. I haaave no-ot brought my-y specs…with…me."

"There was Mag, Mag, looking like a hag," bellowed Mac, "in the store…in the store…"

Before Mac could get any further, Aunt Mag belted out, "There was Mac, Mac, begging for a smack! In the store…in the store!"

Mac roared. It made us all laugh. Then we each had turns.

"There was Evan, Evan, who's just turned eleven, in the store…in the store," sang Pat.

Cedar butted in. "There was Evan, Evan, who can't get into Heaven, in the corner grocery sto-o-ore."

I tried to get him back. "There was Cedar, Cedar, the biggest s'more eater, in the store…in the store…" It was kind of lame, but Cedar laughed anyway.

Peter and Mac sang another song. Their voices fit together. Normally I couldn't care less about music, but their singing made me want to listen. The song was in French, but it didn't matter. It blended with us sitting around a fire in the cold night. After it ended, they got everyone singing. First we sang "Down by the Bay" and "Land of the Silver Birch," then "The Other Day I Met a Bear," which was goofy but funny.

Pat poured everyone some hot chocolate from a thermos. After we'd had more moose cookies, Peter divided us up into three groups and we sang "Row, Row, Row Your Boat" in a round. I felt good singing along.

Then Mac told us a story. "Back when my great-grandfather was a kid, he knew a young man who went deep into the woods of Quebec to apprentice as a logger. It was a cold hard winter that year, oh my." Mac shook his head. Then he frowned. "Maybe I'd better not tell that one," he said.

Cedar grinned and nudged me. "He always does this," he whispered to me.

"DAD!" Kait and Trinnie cried.

"Actually maybe it's too late for a story...some girls may be too young to stay up past their bedtime on account of their grumpiness the next day."

"DAD!" shrieked Trinnie.

"That's not fair!" shouted Kait.

"What do you think, Evan?" Mac asked me. "Do you want to hear the story of the Chasse-galerie?"

"The what?" I said.

"What we call the flying canoe in English," Mac said.

I looked at Cedar. A canoe couldn't fly...could it? But Cedar was nodding like crazy, so I nodded too.

Mac smiled. "Well, as I was saying, it was a long hard winter that year. The days were dark and the nights were so cold your nose would freeze shut and you would die a blackened icicle if you stayed out too long."

Trinnie climbed into Pat's lap.

"Mac!" said Pat in a warning tone.

"Well, it was very cold," said Mac. "And the loggers were working too far back in the bush to be able to get home for the holidays. But as New Year's approached, they grew more and more homesick.

They wished and prayed that they could go home, just for a few hours…and someone heard their prayers. Someone who had terrible plans. This someone appeared at the door on the darkest day and offered them the use of his great canoe…"

Mac sure knew how to tell a story. He kept all of us on the edge of our logs, leaning forward to find out what happened next.

"Some of the loggers made a pact with the shadowy figure at the door," Mac continued. "He offered to let them fly through the night in his magic canoe to see their families at New Year's. In exchange they had to swear an oath not to fly over any church and to be back by sun-up of the next day. He warned them that if they broke their oath, they would owe him their souls. They agreed and then discovered they'd sworn an oath to the devil himself. But the loggers were so homesick that they didn't care. They took off into the sky in the great flying canoe and flew home to their loved ones. They had such a welcome! They danced and they sang and they ate and…they forgot the time. It was only when the night began to fade that they realized their trouble. 'Quick, we must return at once!' They leapt into the canoe. They paddled like madmen across the sky. Just before dawn they tried a shortcut to speed up their arrival to the logging camp. Alas! They took a wrong turn and found themselves swooping over a town, zooming toward a church. 'Head for the trees!' roared their leader, but it was too late!"

Mac stopped the story suddenly and looked around at us. I wanted to shout at him to keep going, but luckily Kait did it for me.

"Go *on*, Dad!" said Kait.

Trinnie's mouth formed a great big O.

"Oh dear," said Mac. "This is a sad tale. It is not really for young ears."

"Dad!" said Cedar.

"Mac, shame on you!" Pat said.

Mac held up his hands, pretending to defend himself. "Okay, okay. But don't say I didn't warn you!" He took a deep, dramatic breath and shook his head. "The canoe scraped over the church spire and the men, unable to do anything about it, cried out in despair. For at that moment they realized their pact was broken. It was the exact moment the devil was waiting for. The canoe bucked and leapt, and then it tipped forward on its nose and plunged down, down and down. The loggers were never seen again.

"And the flying canoe?" said Mac. His eyes were glittery when he looked at me. "Well, they say it is still out there, soaring through the night with the devil at its stern." Mac leaned forward and dropped his voice. So we leaned forward too. "He waits for the next bright soul to fall into his trap. So beware, my friends, beware."

I imagined the canoe leaping through the flames in front of me. I heard the wind whistling through the treetops. Cold crept under my jacket and sucked at my bones. It gave me the creeps thinking that there might be worse than wildlife around here.

Kait was squished up next to Pat and Trinnie, looking spooked.

"Peter, did you call Fish and Wildlife about our loon?" Aunt Mag said. She obviously thought a change of subject was a good idea.

"Yes, I'm waiting for a call back. The bird biologist is away for a couple of days," Peter said.

"I hope he has some answers," said Pat.

Peter scowled. It was the first time I'd seen him look grouchy. "I hope the loon isn't sick." He jabbed the fire with a stick. "People are *still* using lead sinkers to fish with in spite of the regulations."

"What's wrong with lead sinkers?" asked Kait.

"Loons sometimes swallow them," said Aunt Mag.

"Lead is poisonous," said Peter. "One sinker can kill a loon."

Cedar leaned over to me. "We've got a loon that might be in trouble."

"I noticed," I said. "Why is everyone so freaked out about it? It's not like someone's trying to smuggle a loony bird. Maybe living up here in the wilderness has made you all a bit loony." I chuckled.

Cedar didn't laugh. He shrugged. "Whatever," he said. He took out a pocketknife and started shaving his marshmallow stick with short angry strokes.

I realized I'd made him mad. It gave me a heavy feeling in my stomach all of a sudden. I didn't like it. "Sorry," I muttered.

He refused to look at me. I offered him the bag of marshmallows. He shook his head.

"Moose cookie?" I asked.

He shook his head.

I cleared my throat. "Aunt Mag has been talking about the loon ever since I got here."

"Yeah, she does that," Cedar said.

"What *is* the big deal?" I asked. I really wanted to know now. Obviously it wasn't just Aunt Mag. If even Cedar was bothered about it, then maybe there *was* something to think about.

"Loons are cool," said Cedar. "They're sorta mysterious, ya know? Uncle Peter says there used to be more of them on the lake. He's worried they might be disappearing. I guess we're all hoping that this one's all right, is all."

I nodded. "Okay," I said. Maybe there was more to wildlife than I realized. I agreed with Cedar when I thought about it. I remembered the loon checking me out. It *was* cool. "Sorry," I said again.

This time Cedar nodded.

I continued watching him carve his stick.

When he noticed me watching, he handed over the knife. I examined it in the firelight. I'd wanted one for ages. Mom kept telling me I had to wait until I showed more responsibility. I tried it out on my own stick. Pretty soon I had a pointy end, sharp enough to jab through the heart of any hungry spider. I flipped the stick over and did the other end too. Then Cedar said something that made him my friend for the whole rest of my life.

"You can keep that if you want. I've got another one."

I stared at him. No one had ever given me something like this before. I wouldn't have given it away even if I had a hundred pocketknives. "Really?" I said. I looked at it and then at him again. "Thanks!"

"Sure thing." He smiled at me. "Want to get together tomorrow?"

"That'd be awesome!" I said.

CHAPTER 7

The Loneliest Sound

After everyone left, Aunt Mag said, "There's one more thing we need to do tonight." She picked up a couple of the blankets. Unfolding them, she stepped onto the dock and laid them down. What kind of weird thing was she up to now? I wondered. She lay down on her back. She didn't say anything, just patted the space beside her. Feeling kind of dumb, I lay down too.

"Are we going to sleep here?" I asked.

"No," she said. "Look up." The sky curved above us like a black umbrella decorated with a bazillion stars. I felt the night wrap itself around me. It was so quiet. Except for the lights from a couple of houses across the lake, the forest was dark. I'd never seen dark like this at home. I had no idea there were so many stars shining over my head all this time. I filled up my eyes with all those silent shimmers. I heard Aunt Mag's slow breathing. I thought maybe she was asleep, but her eyes were open and she was smiling slightly. Usually grown-ups are in a big hurry to show you stuff and tell you how great it is. Aunt Mag obviously didn't know that's what you were supposed to do, because she didn't do it. I think she had forgotten I was there.

A streak of light shot by overhead.

"Meteor," Aunt Mag said softly.

"Maybe it's the flying canoe," I said.

My aunt chuckled. "You have a vivid imagination," she said, and she sounded like she meant it in a good way.

Then out of the dark a two-note cry rose up through the night. It was the loneliest sound I'd ever heard.

"What's that?" I asked, really glad that my aunt was next to me.

"That's the loon," said Aunt Mag.

"That sound was made by a bird?" I didn't believe her.

"That was one of its four calls. It's what we call the wail. It's like no other sound on earth."

"You're not kidding!" I said. I wouldn't forget that sound anytime soon.

I tried to remember what she told me earlier about it still being here. "Why do you think it's still here if they usually leave sooner?"

I felt her shift beside me. "I wish I knew."

"Isn't it cold out there? I mean, it's freezing." My butt was turning into a buttsicle.

"Loons have lots of blood flowing to their feet. They don't feel the cold the way we do. The males actually arrive the day the ice leaves the lake in the spring. The females follow shortly after. In the fall, some of them—the young ones—sometimes leave just before freeze-up. I don't think they'd have survived thirty million years if they didn't know what they were doing."

I gulped. "That's one old bird."

Aunt Mag laughed. "It's an old species. Our loon is not that old."

"I know that!" I said, though with all the weird things in the wildlife world, you never know.

"Sorry," said Aunt Mag, and she *sounded* sorry.

Then I felt bad. "Is that a young one?" I asked. "Maybe it doesn't know better."

"Judging from its color, no, it's not. The youngsters don't get their adult feathers for a couple of years."

"Then why is this one hanging around?"

"I'm not really sure," said Aunt Mag. "We've had a lot fewer loons on the lake these last few summers. I just hope this one leaves soon or it will be in trouble."

"What will happen?" I asked.

"With this cold, much of the lake will freeze within a couple of days. Loons need at least a hundred and fifty meters of open water to take off."

"Can't they use a tree or something, like normal birds?" I asked.

"They don't move well on land," said Aunt Mag. "Their legs are so far back on their bodies, that it's difficult for them to walk. They don't live in trees the way other birds do. Most birds have hollow bones to make them lighter. Loons have solid bones to make them heavier so they can dive. They really only go on land when they are nesting. The rest of the time they spend in the water. For a loon to get airborne, it takes a lot of effort and a lot of open water. They can't do it from land."

I was quiet, thinking about all this. Aunt Mag sure knew a ton about birds. How did she know it all? Maybe she was a little loopy, but she sure was smart. What would it feel like to have hollow bones so I could fly? Or special eyes so I could hide under water?

"What happens if it can't take off?" I asked finally.

Aunt Mag hesitated, and then she said, "It'll be trapped. Eventually the whole lake will freeze. Once it can't dive for food anymore, it'll starve."

I frowned. "But that won't happen, will it? I mean, if they usually leave, it must know it has to, doesn't it?"

"I hope so," she said, but she didn't sound convinced.

"Can't you do something?" If she knew so much, wouldn't she know how to make it to leave?

"I'm not sure what would work," she said. "It may just be one of those things that happens."

As if it heard her, the loon cried again. I felt like it was calling to me. I got goose bumps thinking about it out there by itself in the cold, dark lake. "You can't let it die!"

Aunt Mag didn't answer for a moment; then she said, "Every living being dies, Evan."

"But you have to try and save it, Aunt Mag! You have to!" I don't know why it mattered so much all of a sudden, but it did. And right then and there I made up my mind to find some way to help. My aunt would help too. She just had to.

CHAPTER 8

Wolves

I was dreaming about being chased in my canoe by a flying weiner with fangs when someone shook me.

"Evan, wake up," Aunt Mag said. "Come outside. Quick!" She disappeared down the loft ladder. I sat up, squinted at the lamp she'd turned on and flopped back on my pillow.

"Hurry up!" she barked from below.

I climbed out of bed and stumbled down the ladder. Aunt Mag held out my jacket. I pulled it on while she jammed a toque on my head. She raced out the door. I managed to get my feet into some boots. I shuffled outside after her. The moon shone through the trees. Cold air smacked me in the face. My aunt grabbed my arm and marched me into the forest.

Suddenly my ears woke up. A long rising howl made the hair stand up all over my body. The howl went on and on and then slowly died out. It was really quiet for a second. Then from far away came an answer. Cries, yips and howls.

Aunt Mag stood there with a goofy smile stuck on her face. "Wolves!" she whispered. We listened and listened while they sang their song. Their voices overlapped, rising and falling through the night. It made me shiver but I hoped it wouldn't stop. They sounded like they were having a party. When the wolves finally did stop howling, Aunt Mag's eyes sparkled.

"I never tire of hearing that sound," she said. She tipped her head back and gave her own howl, long, weird and powerful. A few moments later the wolves answered. My mouth fell open.

"You try it," she said when they had stopped again.

I made an attempt. My voice came out as a croak and ended in a cough.

Aunt Mag jabbed me in the chest with her finger. "You have to mean it!" she said.

So I tried again. I closed my eyes and let loose. I was pleased with the result. It was the best imitation of a wolf that anyone had ever heard.

"What was that?" Aunt Mag demanded. "A cat being tortured or a banshee with the flu?"

Okay, so maybe not the best imitation. We listened. Silence. I tried again. Then Aunt Mag tried, but it was over. The wolves didn't sing again. We trudged back inside.

"Do wolves eat people?" I asked as we hung up our coats.

"Wolves mostly avoid people." Aunt Mag poked the fire in the woodstove and added a piece of wood. We shifted closer to warm up. "The fact is, Evan, when wild animals come into contact with humans, it often goes badly for the animals."

"Is that why you punched that guy and ended up a convict?" I asked.

Aunt Mag turned slowly to look at me.

"I mean," I said. "I didn't mean…"

"I punched the guy because I got mad." She leaned toward me, and I moved away so fast I fell off my chair. She helped me up. "He was getting away with doing things that were wrong. I knew that he'd go on doing those things somewhere else."

"What was it like in the Big House?" I asked.

"'The Big House'?" Her eyebrows practically flew off her head. "Evan, you watch way too much television." She crossed her arms. "It was boring, actually. I sat in a smelly room for two days with one other woman, who either snored her head off or swore at the top of her lungs because she couldn't get a cigarette. The charges were dropped before I even had a hearing." She sighed. "I'm not actually very proud of myself for losing my temper. Socking someone is not a recommended way to resolve an argument." She scrunched up her mouth. "I had all this evidence, you know? Proof that he was taking those turtles illegally." She shook her head. "But he had money to pay for an expensive lawyer. It was the photograph of me punching his lights out that saved the turtle." Her shoulders sagged. "But I was wrong to do it. Violence is not a good way to solve anything."

"It saved the turtles," I said. She nodded but didn't look any happier. "I think it's cool," I went on. "Obviously other people thought so, too, or you might still be in jail. I bet the turtles would thank you if they could. Don't you think being kidnapped and smuggled away is pretty violent?"

Aunt Mag snorted. "Yes, when you put it like that," she said. Then she sighed.

"How come you know so much about turtles and wolves and loons and stuff?" I asked.

She was silent for a moment. "It's my life," she said. "The natural world isn't soft and sweet. It's harsh, and"—her mouth turned up slightly—"it can be violent. But it's also full of life and beauty and extraordinary marvels. And we need those things, Evan. We can learn so much from them." She stopped. Glancing at me, she cleared her throat. "People think I'm a little…extreme. But some of what's out there is disappearing, and I want to learn what I can before it's gone." She turned slightly red and looked away. I nodded. Definitely a little wacky, but she sort of made sense too. "Okay," I said.

She stood up. "Back to bed for you," she growled.

I stood up too. "Thanks for waking me up, Aunt Mag," I said. "Hearing those wolves was awesome."

CHAPTER 9

Alone Again

CRASH. I jerked sideways, fell off the bed and thudded—wide awake—to the floor. My heart whammed in my chest.

"Sorry!" shouted Aunt Mag from below. "No harm done!"

Except I might be having a heart attack. I waited until my breathing returned to normal before I got up. I rubbed away the gunk that had grown in my eyes overnight and went downstairs.

My aunt wore her puffy parka with the duct-tape patches, and a hat with earflaps. She was loading a backpack with tools and weird-looking needles. There was a gun lying on the floor. What was she up to? Was all her talk about beauty and nature and turtles a scam?

"Oh, good, Evan." She smiled at me before continuing to stuff things into the pack. "Listen, I have to go out to work for a couple of hours. I'm really sorry. Something urgent has come up. One of the wolves we've been studying has dropped its radio collar, and there's a big storm coming in tonight."

"You study wolves?" I looked at the gun. "Live wolves?"

She looked puzzled. Then she saw what I was staring at. She laughed. "It's a dart gun. I always carry it in the truck." She picked it up. "We're tracking a wolf pack. We need the data from the collar, and it'll be a lot harder to retrieve it if it gets buried in snow." She put her pack over her shoulder.

I didn't really know what she was talking about, but it sounded pretty interesting.

"The Spencers are just back from church, and Cedar is coming right over to take you to his place. Will you be okay for a few minutes on your own?"

"Sure," I said. "I stay by myself after school if Mom's late from work. But I have a better idea. I'll get dressed and come with you." Maybe this time the wolves would answer me. I rushed to the ladder. This was going to be great.

My aunt's words stopped me halfway up. "I can't take you on this trip. I'm really sorry."

I looked over my shoulder at her. "I could help," I said. "I could hold stuff." Like the gun, I thought. "I won't get in the way."

She was already shaking her head. "Not this time. I have to track a fair way into the bush and it'll be hard for you to keep up."

"But what about all that stuff about us needing nature?" I argued. I dropped back down to the floor. "I mean, I could learn things, useful information about wolves and the wilderness and...I could do a project for school and teach everyone that we have to respect the earth or...or...it will disappear."

My aunt shook her head more firmly. "Sorry," she said. And before I could think of any other reasons, she rushed out the door. A few moments later I heard her truck start. Why did grown-ups do this? When something really cool came up, something interesting, they always said you couldn't be part of it. It sucked. I kicked a pile of books lying on the floor. They flew everywhere in a satisfying mess.

I spotted Aunt Mag's binoculars and suddenly remembered the loon. I raced to the window and scanned the lake. Aunt Mag was right. Most of it was frozen, just like she said it would be. Then I saw it. The loon moved slowly, way out where there was still some open water. I wanted to get a better look.

I ran to the mudroom and grabbed my jacket, mitts and hat and rushed outside. I hurried down to the dock and watched the loon through the binoculars. Everything seemed calm and normal. The loon swam around, turning its head different ways as if it was just curious about the world. A few times it went under but it popped right up again. I looked at the water around it. It wasn't a big space. I couldn't remember exactly how much room Aunt Mag said loons needed to take off, but it had sounded like a lot. The open water wasn't exactly what I called a lot. That was bad. The loon might look happy now but soon it was going to be in trouble. Big trouble. I took the binoculars away from my eyes.

Would it hurt if you died from starvation? Would it take a long time? I didn't want to think about it. I couldn't. My chest ached. I didn't want the loon to die.

That was when I got the idea. I looked back at the house and then out at the lake. I'd need a few supplies, but I knew my plan would work. I was going to rescue the loon.

CHAPTER 10

Rescue

I ran back to the house and got dressed. I was going to have to get the loon to come out of the water, but how? What did birds eat? Worms! It was going to be a bit hard to find worms in the ground seeing as how it was frozen harder than concrete. Birdseed, that was it. Aunt Mag must have some around. There was a bird feeder hanging outside. Where'd she keep the seed? I dashed into the kitchen and opened all the cupboards. No luck. Maybe outside? I wished Cedar was here, because I was sure he'd know. I thought about waiting for him, but everyone knows that if you are waiting for something it takes a hundred times longer for it to happen.

Outside, all I found near the house was a metal garbage can full of gray dust that blew up into my face.

It smelled like the smoke from Aunt Mag's chimney. Coughing, I clapped the lid back on. Whatever it was, it wasn't birdseed.

I spotted the two-story garage. There must be something in there a loon could eat. I ran over and heaved on the garage door handle. The door groaned, but I managed to push it up. Inside, I looked around, surprised. No wonder Aunt Mag didn't keep her truck in here. It was crammed full of junk. Her habit of keeping everything insanely tidy sure didn't apply to her garage. This was more like it. Cedar and I could have tons of fun in here.

I saw a door with a sign on it that said: *DO NOT ENTER*. I shoved it open. I felt for the light switch and flipped it up. A weak lightbulb flickered on. Bottles with hard-to-read labels sat on shelves above a metal counter. Boxes and large packages were stuffed underneath. There were tools that looked like something a doctor or a dentist would use. The room was obviously some kind of lab. Did Aunt Mag do experiments or something? Curious, I pulled open the little fridge. There were a few small bottles with rubber tops. Two of them had crusty dribbles down their sides. There was also a big brown glass jar that was half full of liquid.

I opened it and nearly barfed. It stank like the worst case of farts I've ever smelled. Worse even than when my friend Henry eats too much cheese. I closed it fast, trying not to breathe. What kind of lab was this? Unfortunately the smell lingered up my nose, and I had to plug my nostrils with some paper towel that I found above the small sink. This wasn't helping me find birdseed.

More cautiously, I opened the one tall cupboard. A zombie lunged out at me, and I yelled my head off. I stopped yelling when I realized it was just some dirty old coveralls that had fallen off their hook. High up on a shelf in one corner I spotted some bones. I dragged a stool over and climbed up. It was an animal skull. I lifted it down and turned it all around. One of the pointy teeth fell out in my hand. Even without eyeballs, the eye sockets stared at me. It made me feel sick so I put the whole thing back in a hurry. I climbed down off the stool. What did Aunt Mag *do* in here? Finally I looked more carefully under the counter. I found a bin with a cartoon picture of a bird on the side. I lifted the top. Bull's-eye! It was full to the brim with birdseed.

I scooped some seed into a paper bag I found on top of the fridge. That ought to keep the loon happy for the trip across the lake. But how would I carry it? I went into the other part of the garage and found an old sled and a wooden box half filled with straw. Perfect.

By the time I got everything down to the beach, I was sweating. It had taken me longer than I expected to get everything together, and I was impatient to get going. I took another look through the binoculars. The loon was still there, swimming about in the open water.

I stepped out onto the frozen lake and fell on my butt. I got up, rubbing the sore spot. I headed for open water, being careful not to slip. The wind blew in my face. The sun was so bright that I had to squint every time I looked up. The box kept slipping off the sled, so I used some of the long pull rope to tie it on.

I thought I heard a shout from behind me. I looked back at the shore. I didn't realize how far I'd come already.

"Evan!" Cedar was jumping up and down, waving his arms like a maniac. I waved back.

"Hi!" I yelled.

Cedar shouted something. The wind blew away his words.

"What?" I shouted.

"…the ice!" was all I heard.

"What?" I yelled again.

Cedar shouted again. Again the wind blew away his words.

"I'm going to rescue the loon!" I shouted back, but Cedar was pelting away from the shore up the path.

The ice near where I was walking groaned. I froze to the spot and looked down. *Crack.* My foot went through. I jumped back. Water splashed up from a foot-sized hole where I'd been standing. I backed away. Another piece of ice disappeared. Black water grabbed at my feet. I kept stepping backward. Each time, the ice held just long enough for me to take another step back, and then it sank. I looked over my shoulder at the shore in panic. Cedar was back. Aunt Mag was barreling down the path and onto the beach. She hollered something, but I couldn't understand the words. Peter and Mac followed on her heels. *Crack.* What was I going to do? My legs shook, but I had to keep stepping back so the water wouldn't catch me. It kept spurting up as each hole opened.

"Evan!" It was Peter's voice. "Lie…sled!"

I couldn't hear properly in the wind. He wanted me to lie on the sled? Why? I stepped back again. This time the ice held.

"Lie…the sled," Peter cried again.

But what if the whole lake cracked open and swallowed me up? I imagined the ice-cold water sucking me under. What if I couldn't find the surface? The darkness underneath would hold me down until I ran out of air. I felt weak. I couldn't move.

"Evan! Listen…Peter!" Aunt Mag's voice sounded high and screechy.

Peter called something. It sounded like he was trying to explain something. My aunt had said to listen to Peter. So I shut my eyes and tried to listen over the sound of my thumping heart and the wind.

"…spread weight…over the surface…safer."

He wanted me to lie down to spread out my weight? But I'd have to untie the box and if I even took one step the ice might break. I looked at the shore again. It wasn't any closer. Peter pushed a black floppy thing onto the lake.

"You can…Evan!" Peter didn't sound scared like Aunt Mag. He just sounded like he knew what I should do.

Slowly I crouched down. The ice creaked but it held. I had a hard time with the knots. I couldn't feel my fingers all that well anymore, but I got one side of the box untied. Without a sound the ice under me sank. I threw myself onto the sled. Birdseed spilled everywhere. The box hurt my stomach but the sled reached across the gap of water. My heart pounded.

"Hang on, Evan." Peter's voice was clearer and closer.

I opened my eyes and looked back. Peter lay flat on a floppy rubber boat. He pushed himself forward using his hands.

"Just stay put, buddy. Okay?"

I nodded. There was another creak and my sled dropped at the front end. Please let Peter get here. Please.

And then he was. A strong tug pulled the sled back. "Stay still for a moment. I know it's uncomfortable but I'm going to back us up a bit onto thicker ice. Okay?"

I nodded again. I swallowed hard and fast and tried to ignore the hammering in my chest. I clung on to the sled underneath me. Peter eased us back and back. I tried to get my breathing under control.

Then we stopped. Firm hands lifted me off the sled. I was shaking. Peter pulled me into his lap like I was a little kid, but I didn't care. I hung on to him for all I was worth. I felt all rubbery and I couldn't stop shivering. My chest hurt. I wanted to cry.

"You're okay, Evan. I've got you and you're safe." Peter's arms wrapped around me. I closed my eyes and rested my head against his jacket. The two of us sat until I could breathe again.

"I'm sorry," I whispered.

"I know," he said. "You wanted to help the loon, didn't you?"

I nodded.

"Your aunt said you did. She could tell it was important to you. We were talking about what to do about it."

I lifted my head. "She said it would die. She said it happened sometimes. I think she was going to let it. She says she loves animals. Why would she save turtles and not a loon?"

"It's not that simple, Evan."

I didn't understand. Not one bit. "But why wouldn't we help it if we can?"

Peter sighed. Then he hugged me. "Come on," he said. "Let's get you back to the shore before Mag tries to come out here too."

CHAPTER 11

The Promise

Aunt Mag nearly crushed me in a hug when we got back to shore. Her face was so white that her freckles stood out on her skin like a spotty disease. She didn't say anything. She just looked at me and then squashed me against her again. For once Cedar was quiet. Kait and Trinnie stood a little behind him and stared at me. Mac wrapped a blanket around me, but his expression made me glad Aunt Mag's arm was around my shoulder.

"You were lucky this time, Evan," said Mac in a low voice. "You couldn't have been expected to know before, but now you do. You are *never* to go out onto the ice without an adult. Do you understand?" He clenched his hands by his sides. I swallowed hard and nodded. "Not *ever*!" he said even louder.

Peter put a hand on his arm. "It's okay, Mac," he said.

Mac stepped back. The look on his face made me shiver. He turned away and led the girls up the path without another word.

"Something hot to drink would be in order," said Peter.

Aunt Mag didn't let go of me until we reached the door to the house.

"Cedar, why don't you and I make some tea," said Peter.

"Okay," said Cedar. He glanced at me and then followed his uncle inside. Peter shut the inner door behind them. My aunt sank down on the bench in the mudroom.

"I should never have left you alone," she said in a choked voice.

"I'm okay though," I said.

Her face was all screwed up like she was trying not to cry. "You were lucky that Cedar saw you when he did," she said. "When I think of what might have happened…" She pinched her lips together. Her chin wobbled.

"But I got rescued," I said. "I'm fine. Look," I said, trying to make her feel better. "I've got all my arms and legs."

"Evan, this isn't some kind of *joke*! You could have *drowned*! Do you know that? You could be dead. *Right now*! This isn't something to laugh about." She blew a big breath out. "Oh, Evan." She closed her eyes and shook her head.

A big lump rose in my throat. I sat down beside her. "Sorry, Aunt Mag," I said. "I didn't think about the ice. I just wanted to help the loon."

"We *all* want to help the loon, Evan, but there are ways to go about it that are not so dangerous," she said. "None of us want to see it die."

"But you made it sound like you might let it," I said.

Aunt Mag sighed. "We may not be able to prevent that from happening. Even if we're able to rescue it, there is no guarantee it will survive." She rubbed her hand over her eyes. "Loons are..." She paused. "They're wild spirits. They don't do well around humans. We may harm it just by rescuing it."

"But you said it would die for sure if it's trapped here. Can't we try and save it?"

Aunt Mag nodded. "We're going to. Mac has a friend with the phone company and they have a hovercraft. He's going to ask if they'd be willing to help."

"That's awesome!" I said. "It's perfect. It'll work. I'm sure it'll work. Can we call the guy now?"

"Mac put in a call to him early this morning."

"So you do want to help!" I said. I knew it. My aunt wouldn't let a loon die if she could help it.

She pulled off her boots and got to her feet. She looked serious. "I just don't want you to get your hopes up, Evan. This may not work."

But I was sure it would.

She rested her hand on the doorknob to the hallway. "Years ago, Peter and Mac lost a brother through the ice. He was seventeen. He took a snowmobile out on the lake and hit a rotten spot. By the time they got to him, there was no way to save him. He got caught under the ice, and they couldn't get him out in time. You were lucky today. *Extremely* lucky. Everyone around here has a healthy respect for the lake. The ice is off-limits. Do you understand?"

I nodded. I remembered the water sucking at my feet. I felt all rubbery again thinking about it.

"Promise me you will not go out on the lake again without my permission." She looked me straight in the eye.

I looked straight back. "I promise, Aunt Mag." And I really, really meant it.

CHAPTER 12

A Respected Scientist

Aunt Mag went off to get changed. Peter poured me some tea. I dumped four heaping spoonfuls of sugar into my cup and filled the rest of the space up with milk. Peter didn't say anything. Mom would've had a fit about all that sugar. But she wasn't here. It tasted good. It helped the rubbery feeling go away.

Cedar was looking at me like I had an extra head.

"Good thing you got back when you did," I said to him.

"Good thing Uncle Peter was here," he said. "Boy, were you dumb! You gotta wait a few cold days for the ice to get thick. You wait until the ice fishermen bring their huts out; then you're safe."

"You wait until you have a grown-up with you who knows what they're doing!" said Peter.

"Yeah, that's what I meant," said Cedar, shrinking down a little in his chair.

I had sure picked the wrong mistake to make here. "I'm really sorry, Mr. Spencer," I said. I really meant it. I wanted him to see that.

"Mr. Spencer?" Cedar burst out laughing.

Peter cuffed him lightly on the side of the head. "That's *Doctor* Spencer to you, young nephew," he said. He looked at me. "You won't make the mistake about the ice again, will you?" His didn't let go of my gaze until I shook my head. I remembered about his brother. His and Mac's.

"If we have to start calling you 'Doctor Spencer,' do we have to start calling Evan's Auntie Mag 'Doctor Kemp'?" Cedar asked.

I spewed out my tea. "Aunt Mag? A doctor?"

"She's a wildlife biologist, Evan. A very well-respected scientist with a PhD. She's a leading expert on the eastern wolf," Peter said.

My aunt? The ex-con? A respected scientist? No way. But Peter was serious. I realized my mouth was hanging open, so I closed it. "Aunt Mag is full of surprises," I said.

Peter chuckled. "Yes, she is," he said. His eyes twinkled. "Did you know she was always getting into trouble when she was your age?"

I shook my head.

"Yep," continued Peter. "She was worse than your dad. She could never turn down a dare. There was this one time when—"

"Uncle Peter," interrupted Cedar. "How about you save the good-old-days stories for another time? I'm starving."

My stomach must have been listening, because right then it let out a ripping growl. "Me too," I said as they both laughed.

Cedar nipped over to the fridge and pulled out a package of cheddar. "Can we have grilled cheese?"

Peter nodded. "Good idea."

Aunt Mag came back and sank into a chair. Peter handed her a mug of tea. Her hand shook a little as she added milk. Cedar and I glanced at each other. Peter reached into a cupboard and lifted out a bottle of some golden liquid. He unscrewed the lid and glugged some into Aunt Mag's tea. She took a gulp. Then another one. She started to look a little less freaked. "Are you making grilled cheese?" she asked Peter. He nodded. "Will you make me one?" she asked.

"Sure thing. Cedar, would you slice some more cheese?" Peter said.

The phone rang and my aunt went to answer it. A few moments later she came back looking much happier. "They picked up the collar," she said.

"Good," said Peter as he flipped over the sandwich in the frying pan with one smooth toss.

Cedar grabbed the frying pan and tried flipping. Peter caught the sandwich on a plate before it fell to the floor. He gave Cedar a look that I was beginning to recognize as the Spencer warning look. Cedar sat back down like a scolded dog.

"The wolf collar?" I asked. "The one you were going to pick up this morning?"

"I was heading that way," she said, "but partway down the road, I started to worry about leaving you on your own. I called one of my students. He said he'd go for me." She gulped down more tea. "As it turned out, I was right to be worried. I got back right when Cedar came up from the lake, hollering for help."

"Oh," I said. No one else said anything. I felt my face get hot.

Peter turned off the stove and set the plate of sandwiches on the table. "I cooked, so you boys can clean up. I have to get going. See if the two of you can stay out of trouble for the rest of the day, okay?" We both nodded.

Aunt Mag stood up as he put on his jacket. "Peter…," she said.

"It's all right, Mag." He gave her a quick smile. Before she could say anything else he slipped out the door.

CHAPTER 13

The Best Woodpile in the County

Aunt Mag set Cedar and me to work stacking fire-wood. At first it was fun. We took turns pushing the wheelbarrow. We turbo-blasted the loads over to where we were stacking it. When that got boring, we pushed each other. Then we made a track. We had an awesome obstacle course set up when Aunt Mag came out to inspect our pile.

"Working hard, I see," she said.

"It *was* hard to get that slope just right," said Cedar, pointing at the jump we'd made out of junk from the garage.

Aunt Mag took in the jump and then me in the wheelbarrow. She eyed the measly amount of wood we'd stacked. "Well," she said, "good thing you didn't get too far because what you did will have to be done over."

Cedar groaned.

"What?" I said. "No way!"

"Yes way," she said. "This'll never hold up a full woodpile, and if it falls over and sits there, it'll rot." She kicked the pile. The whole thing collapsed. "You, at least, ought to know better, Cedar."

"Why is it always my fault?" Cedar demanded. "'You should know better, Cedar. You're the oldest, so you have to set a good example, Cedar.' Ugh!" He looked so disgusted that Aunt Mag laughed.

"Come on, guys, I'll help get you started." I climbed out of the wheelbarrow and watched. She showed us how to make the ends strong. First she put down two pieces of firewood facing the same way with a space between. Then she put two more on top going across the other way.

"Keep stacking pieces like that, alternating the direction each time until you've built the stack up fairly high," said Aunt Mag. "Once you've made a tower like that at each end, you fill in the middle in straight rows." She gestured at the pile. "Go to it." She sounded way too cheerful.

Cedar and I built the towers up until Aunt Mag said they were high enough. Then we stacked wood until I was sure my arms would drop off.

"This is what happens when you screw up," Cedar muttered to me while Aunt Mag's back was turned. "They don't give you a time-out. Oh no!" he shook his head. "They make you work! Child labor."

"There are laws against that," I said quietly. "Maybe we could sue."

"Yeah," said Cedar, brightening up. "She's used to jail. What's a little more time in the slammer?"

"What are you two going on about?" asked Aunt Mag, suddenly hanging over us like some kind of fairy-tale ogre.

"Nothing," I said. I picked up more wood. Cedar did too.

"Good," said Aunt Mag. "I thought maybe you were complaining again."

"We've been doing this for hours," I said.

Aunt Mag put her fists on her hips. "Evan, it's been about half an hour, not counting the time you were riding in the wheelbarrow. If we get this done quickly, then we'll have time for the shinny game that's planned for this afternoon."

"Yes!" Cedar pumped the air.

"But," said Aunt Mag, "we have to get this done first. We're expecting heavy snow tonight."

With Aunt Mag helping, it didn't take too long. She barked out orders and threw her hands up in the air if we didn't get each piece exactly straight, but she worked too. She carried huge loads and placed them on the pile so they fit exactly. Cedar was pretty good at it too, I had to admit. He was almost as fast as Aunt Mag. We kind of got a rhythm going. They did two loads; I did one. When we finished, we stood back. Our woodpile was the best one in the whole county, I was sure. It was neat and even, and it didn't fall over when I kicked it. I was getting the hang of this country living.

"Okay, let's go and get our gear," she said.

"What about skates?" I asked.

"I'll go find you some," said Cedar. He bolted off through the woods toward his house.

Aunt Mag chuckled. "You two seem to be getting along like a house on fire," she said.

"He gave me a pocketknife last night!" I blurted out. Then I wish I hadn't. I waited for the lecture about unsafe tools.

"Oh," was all she said. "Nice." She walked off to the house. I stood there and stared after her. I just couldn't figure her out. My mom would have flipped out and taken the knife away from me.

When I went to get on my snow pants, Aunt Mag handed me a hockey stick. "Will this work?"

I hefted it. It felt good. It was old and a bit beat-up, but it felt right in my hand. "Yep," I said.

"It was your dad's," she said as we headed out the door again. "He was one of the best players on the lake."

I grasped it more tightly. I suddenly wished he was here. I swallowed. "Could we call Dad later?" I asked.

Aunt Mag nodded. "I was planning on calling him tonight anyway. He and your mom need to know about what happened on the lake."

"You don't have to tell him," I said. "Nothing really happened. Besides, it wasn't your fault."

She stopped so suddenly that I smacked right into her. "Yes, it was, Evan. I shouldn't have left you alone."

"I'm not a little kid," I protested. "I stay home alone all the time."

"I know, but still. You're used to the city. Things work a little differently around here. There are certain basic things that have to do with safety that you don't know."

"I'm trying to learn," I said.

She looked at me. Something in her face was hard for me to look at. It was like she was seeing inside me: the good stuff and the not so good. And she still thought I was okay.

"I was terrified by what could have happened to you out there, Evan. I also understood why you did it. At your age, I would have tried the same stupid thing." She adjusted the skates hanging around her neck. "I'm responsible for you. Your dad needs to know. Okay?"

I nodded.

"Okay," she said. "Let's go show those Spencers how to play hockey."

CHAPTER 14

Victory

Smoke puffed out of the Spencers' chimney. I sniffed the air. It smelled great. Cedar galloped up to me and led me around behind their house. I stopped in my tracks and stared at a huge oval rink with smooth ice. Humongous logs with seats carved into them lined the edges. A net stood at each end.

"Cedar, it's awesome!" I said.

"Really?" said Cedar. "I thought maybe you'd think it was lame 'cause you're used to city rinks."

"No way. It's so cool." I wanted one. My backyard at home wasn't big enough. That's what you get in the city. No room for fun.

Cedar grinned. "Come on." He pulled me over to a bunch of other kids putting on skates. They were all friendly. There were a couple of grown-ups apart from Pat, Mac and Aunt Mag. Cedar handed me some skates. I put them on, and we glided onto the ice. A happy feeling the size of the universe filled me up. I zoomed backward and forward all over the rink.

Cedar joined me with another boy named Ravi. Cedar pointed to a smaller kid having his skates tied by Pat. "That's Ravi's brother, Harsha. Don't be fooled by his size." Ravi grinned and gave Cedar a high five.

"Listen up!" Mac shouted. "We're going to pick teams. Everyone gather up."

Picking teams, I found out, meant Mac yelling out names and then pointing to one end of the rink or the other, where team members met up. Out of the grown-ups only Aunt Mag and Mac were playing. Aunt Mag was on my team and so were Kait, Trinnie and an older kid named Andrew. Cedar was on the opposite team.

The puck dropped. I flew up the rink. No one spoke. Sticks clacked together and thwacked against the puck. We played fast and hard. I played for all I was worth. We all did. You could feel it. There was a buzzy feeling in the air.

It seemed like no time at all had passed when Mac called the last ten minutes. My heart pounded, and I was panting. Mac offered to let me have a rest. Everyone else had taken a turn off the ice, but I shook my head. I swiped the sweat out of my eyes. Mac put me in center. I stood face-to-face with a girl named Jenny who was a lot bigger than me. She was good too. It was going to be tough to get the puck away from her once she had it. The score was tied. Little snowflakes were falling and it was starting to get dark.

I was pumped as I waited for the puck to drop. This was it. This was going to be my moment. I felt it. *Plop.* Before I could move, Jenny scooped the puck away. She skated like a demon and knocked the puck around Andrew and then Aunt Mag. She set up for a pass to Cedar, who had a clear shot on the net. I bent my head and raced forward. I reached her just as she smacked the puck. It ricocheted off the end of my stick. Yes! Trinnie skated out of nowhere and picked it up. She slid between her father's legs on her stomach, pushing the puck to her sister. Kait wound up to shoot. Her aim was wonky. Jenny caught the puck and passed it to Harsha who zoomed away. The puck flew down the rink, passing from player to player. They were going to score.

My legs ached as I burned up the rink. Andrew tripped over Kait and went down, but his arm stopped the puck. I picked it up on my stick and flew back up the ice. Mac waited in the middle in front of Ravi, who hovered in goal. Mac smiled in an evil way. I kept my expression cool. He reached out his long arm to take the puck. I watched Ravi behind him. His face told me he was sure Mac would get the puck. He waited slightly to the side, watching for my defeat. It was all I needed. I deked around Mac to the other side. Out of the corner of my eye I saw Mac's smile turn to amazement. And Ravi couldn't move fast enough. I aimed. I shot. I scored!

Everyone went crazy. I thought I was going to burst. The whole group was cheering me. Both teams. Mac heaved me onto his shoulders. Aunt Mag hollered and pumped the air with her stick. Cedar yelled. Kait shrieked. Andrew grinned. Jenny was laughing, and Ravi and Harsha thumped each other on the backs.

Mac lifted me down. "Well played, Evan! Nice to see you keeping up the family tradition."

I grinned and thumped with everyone else.

"Ha!" said Aunt Mag as she came up. "Take that, Mackenzie Spencer."

"I was surprised to see you on the ice today," Mac said to her. "At your age, you ought to be careful."

I thought she might explode. Her face turned a bunch of shades of red, but she took a huge breath, stuck her nose in the air and said, "Well, sometimes it's good for you Johnny-come-latelies to see how real hockey players do it."

I swear you could've heard Mac's bellow of a laugh across the lake. Pat brought out some hot chocolate. We all hung around for a little while longer. Then Aunt Mag said, "Come on, Evan, we better head home. The snow's coming down fast."

"Oh, hey, Mag," called Mac. "Phil called. They're bringing the hovercraft over tomorrow afternoon."

As I walked home with my aunt, I couldn't decide what I was happier about: the hockey game or the loon rescue. Either way, it was victory.

CHAPTER 15

The Hovercraft

The men finally arrived, towing the hovercraft on a trailer behind their big pickup truck. Cedar and I rushed up to look at it while Mac introduced Aunt Mag to the two men. The hovercraft was bright yellow with the phone-company logo painted on the side. It had a windshield, a roof and plastic windows along the sides like a big motorboat. A huge fan covered in a cage sat on the back. I peeked through a side window. There were handlebars to steer with and a long skinny seat running up the middle.

One of the men saw me looking and smiled. "Like it?" he asked.

"I really do!"

He laughed. "You're going to have to move back while we get it started, okay?" He picked up a big helmet and put it on. He and the other man unhitched the trailer from the truck and turned it. They tilted the trailer forward until it touched the ground and then unlatched it.

"Cool, eh?" Cedar said in my ear.

"Sure is!" I was itching to jump in and check out the controls. "It's smaller than I thought." It looked like only two people could fit inside it. Perfect for Cedar and me. We looked at each other and I knew he was thinking the same thing.

Aunt Mag caught our look. "Don't get any ideas," she said firmly. Sheesh.

Cedar and I backed away as one of the men climbed into the hovercraft. It started with a big roar. It sounded like a leaf blower that thought it was a propeller plane. I covered my ears.

"It's loud!" Cedar yelled.

"Yeah!" I yelled back.

Other people drifted up to watch. Andrew and Jenny waved at us. Then I saw Ravi and Harsha and their dad.

The telephone man drove the hovercraft down off the trailer. It really did hover above the ground.

The other guy climbed in and sat on the seat behind the driver. They headed for the lake. We ran after them down to the beach. At the edge of the lake, Aunt Mag handed one of the men a cardboard box and a blanket and did a lot of shouting and pointing. I figured she was explaining how to catch the loon when they got close.

The driver gave a thumbs-up signal. I looked out through my binoculars to where I knew the open water was. I couldn't see much through the falling snow but I knew the loon was there.

The hovercraft zoomed onto the lake. Snow blew up behind.

"Crikey!" Aunt Mag said. "They sure aren't wasting any time, are they?"

"I didn't know it could go that fast," said Pat, coming closer with the girls.

"Since it's off the ground, there's less friction. It takes less effort to make it move," said Mac. He looked as excited as any of us kids.

"I wish I could ride on it," I said.

"Me too," said Cedar. "Boy, oh, boy. Do you think they'd give us a ride?"

"I'm quite sure they've got better things to do than spend the day giving people rides," said Aunt Mag.

"Better for who?" Cedar demanded.

"Whom," said Aunt Mag.

"Whom, shmoom," muttered Cedar.

"It *does* look like fun though," said Pat.

The hovercraft shrank to a teeny yellow blob and then the engine grew louder as the blob turned back into a hovercraft. "Hey, they're coming back!" I yelled.

"Something must have happened," said Aunt Mag.

"Maybe they rescued the loon!" I said.

Aunt Mag shook her head. "Too quick."

Halfway back to shore, the engine suddenly died. The men moved around in the hovercraft.

"Uh-oh," Cedar said.

"What happens without the air?" I asked.

Aunt Mag shrugged. "It's designed to go over water too, so they'll be fine. They'll have to get it going again though. We can't go and help them with the ice being the way it is." The hovercraft coughed and then roared alive. I cheered with Cedar.

The men came back to the shore. More shouting with Aunt Mag. More pointing, and then they raced off again, this time straight toward the loon hole.

"Engine trouble," Aunt Mag called to us. "And they couldn't see the open water."

Way off in the distance the hovercraft sounded like a buzzing bee. We waited. And waited. It took forever. What were they *doing*? Finally it headed back to the beach. I ran over with Aunt Mag. The men shook their heads.

"No sign of the loon. Must have gone under when it heard us coming," shouted one of the men. "There's not much of a hole there now, but I guess it's enough for the bird to hide. Not a lot we can do while it can still dive." They took the hovercraft back to the truck.

Everyone trudged after them except me. They were giving up? No, they couldn't! I ran onto the dock and looked through the binoculars. All I saw was falling snow.

"Come on, Evan," Cedar called. He waited at the bottom of the path.

But I didn't want to. My feet were numb and my face was frozen stiff, but I couldn't leave. I stood on the dock and looked out across the lake. Cedar came up beside me. I knew the loon was out there. Was it okay? Was it scared?

I heard footsteps behind us. Aunt Mag walked onto the dock. "It's a shame. I should have thought of the fact that the loon would dive when they approached. I'm sorry."

"Maybe they could come back and try again when the lake is frozen over," Cedar said.

"Maybe," she said but she didn't sound as if she thought it would happen.

I didn't say anything. Cedar threw a snowball onto the lake and then scooped up more snow to make another one.

"What do we do now?" I asked. "We can't just give up."

"There's a woman I know who is a bird specialist. She might have some ideas. I'll give her a call."

Cedar stopped throwing snowballs and looked hopefully at Aunt Mag.

"Can we call her now?" I asked.

"Don't see why not," said Aunt Mag.

I punched the air and whooped. Cedar let out a holler.

Aunt Mag followed us up the path. "There's no guarantee…"

I'd heard that warning before. But it was better than nothing, which was all we had a few minutes ago.

CHAPTER 16

It's So Not Fair

Cedar kept twitching in his chair as if his underwear was on fire while Aunt Mag called the bird expert. I tried to follow the conversation. All I heard was "Uh-huh," and "Right" and "Okay." Hardly useful information.

"She says there's no point trying a rescue until the hole closes," said Aunt Mag when she got off the phone. "As long as the loon can dive for food, it should be okay. In the meantime we've got to be patient."

"That sucks," said Cedar.

"Yeah. Can't we do something else?" I asked.

"At least she said it'll be all right for now," said Aunt Mag. "Now, you two will have to amuse your-selves for a while. I've got some work to do."

I thought if I had to wait anymore, I was going to explode, but Cedar had tons of ideas to keep us busy so I wasn't bored for even a second. For one thing, he had an awesome collection of comics, and I really got into them. He also had a book about how to draw your own comic. So we made one called "The Fantastic Adventures of Hockey Man and Loof Boy." Hockey Man was a regular guy who could morph into a powerful action man in bullet-proof underwear. He saved people with his superior hockey skills.

Hockey Man's trusty sidekick was Loof Boy. He had a loon's head and wings on a wolf's body. He suffered from stinky dog breath because he smoked too many cigars. He was always trying to quit. In spite of his smelly breath he had many talents, including expert camouflage abilities and a voice that could freeze the blood in people's veins. He was Hockey Man's best and most loyal friend. Together they saved civilization from the evil Lord Bowel and his devious wife Lady Prune who wanted to rule the world. Planning out the story and drawing the pictures took us a long time. Before we knew it, it was time for dinner and then for bed.

The next day Peter and Mac took Cedar and me snow-mobiling. I wore a puffy snowsuit like Cedar's with a thick pair of boots and a balaclava. I pulled on water-proof mittens and a helmet too. I felt like I was dressed to visit the moon.

I climbed on the big machine behind Mac. He started the engine. "Hold on tight," he bellowed over the noise, and then we were flying. Mac took us into the woods. Peter and Cedar followed us. Mac dodged around bushes and humps of rock. It was a bit crazy, but I could tell he knew what he was doing.

We crossed the road and zoomed onto a trail. Mac pointed out two deer leaping away. Their tails flipped white as they disappeared. We wound through the woods. I loved feeling the swoops and bumps. I grinned all the way. Mac sometimes leaned really far over to swing us around a curve. I held on tight so I didn't fly off. The snowmobile roared and whined and farted out a sweetish gas smell that I liked.

After a while, Mac slowed down. We came out of the trees high up on a hill. I could see forever in every direction. Peter pulled up beside us. He and Mac both killed the engines. We all lifted off our helmets, and I pulled up my balaclava like they did too. Peter was smiling at me.

"That was so cool!" I said. And then and there I knew I wanted a snowmobile of my own more than anything else. More than a loft or a hockey rink or even a hovercraft. Maybe I'd even move up here to the wilderness so I could own one.

Mac stepped off the machine and stomped through the soft snow to look down on the view. I slid forward and wrapped my hands around the handlebars and gripped the throttle.

"Hey, Evan, come on over here. You can see the lake," Mac said.

The lake spread out flat below us, wide and white. Sunlight sparkled off the snow. I could see over the treetops. I suddenly imagined what it would look like, sailing across the sky in the flying canoe. Peter pulled out some mini field glasses and peered through them. Then he passed them to me.

"You can see our friend the loon, out there. It still has a little water around it. It's keeping it open by swimming. It won't be able to do that for much longer."

The loon looked like a tiny bump in a small black pool. "What happens when the hole closes?" I asked.

"Then we have to get to it pretty soon. It won't be able to get food and water, and it'll be vulnerable to predators. It'll have a hard time protecting itself."

I took the binoculars away from my eyes. "What do you mean?"

"He means something's gonna eat it if we don't pick it up," said Cedar, taking a turn with the binoculars.

"What?" I said. I couldn't believe it. "Then we have to get there first," I said.

"We have to wait for the ice to be safe enough to walk on," said Mac.

"But that's the same for whatever wants to eat it, isn't it?" I looked at Peter, then Mac.

"Some predators fly, Evan, and many are lighter than a human being," Peter said.

I felt sick thinking about the loon trying to fight off a bunch of eagles or, worse, Aunt Mag's wolves. It couldn't run away or fly or anything. "It's so not fair!" I said. "I can't believe we waited and waited and now you're saying we still may not be able to rescue it. It's not fair!"

"We'll keep our fingers crossed," said Peter. He and Mac walked back to the snowmobiles. The day was ruined. Why hadn't the stupid loon flown away when it was supposed to? Then I wouldn't be in this mess.

Mac started the snowmobile. I climbed on behind him. I couldn't stop thinking about the loon, until Mac stopped on the straight part of the trail.

"Do you want to drive, Evan?" he shouted.

He didn't have to ask me again. He sat behind me, put his hands over mine and showed me how to speed up and slow down and how to stop. Then he let me drive. Cedar got to drive too. At first I went slowly, getting a feel for it, but pretty soon we were whizzing along, flashing by the trees. A big rabbit darted across the trail ahead of us. It was gone in a second. Aunt Mag told me after I got back that it was a snowshoe hare. There sure was a lot of wildlife for a snowy day. Aunt Mag laughed when I said that.

"It's all around us," she said. "You just have to know how to find it."

Then I told Aunt Mag about the predator problem.

"We'll keep a close eye on the loon," she said.

But would that be good enough? I guess I must have looked worried, because she added, "How about we invite Cedar to spend the night?"

I didn't think about the loon at all after that…until the next day.

CHAPTER 17

A Dumb Idea

I woke up to sunlight pouring in the windows. Cedar was snoring his head off, so I decided to let him sleep. I moseyed down to the kitchen, wondering where Aunt Mag was. The house was really quiet. Maybe she was outside. I yawned and glanced out the window. A red bird landed on the bird feeder. Mom had shown me these birds in the city. What had she called them? Cardinals. The bird saw me through the window and tipped its head, turning its eye to me. Then I remembered the *other* bird and I grabbed the binoculars. It took me a few moments to locate it. Oh no! The loon sat on top of the ice. The hole had closed. And something bad was happening. The loon was being attacked. A smaller black bird jumped at it and pecked at its head. The loon opened its wings and lunged at its attacker. But two more black birds dove at it from behind. Another one stood on the ice a few feet away. The loon tried to turn and protect itself. It fell over before it could get close. It struggled to stand again.

"Aunt Mag!" I ran through the house. She wasn't anywhere inside. I opened the door and yelled. No answer. Then I saw her note on the table. *Evan and Cedar, I've gone to pick up an injured wolf that was hit by a car early this morning. I'm sorry to leave you on your own, but it was urgent and I thought you'd be happier if I let you sleep. I left a message with Cedar's parents to let them know what's going on. I know you will both behave responsibly. Call me on my cell if you need me. I'm not too far. I will be back as soon as I can. Mag.* I called her cell phone, but it rang and rang, and then I got a message saying her mailbox was full.

I took another look through the binoculars. The black birds were still there. I raced to the loft and shook Cedar awake. "We've got a big problem!"

Cedar rubbed his eyes and sat up in bed. He blinked a few times. "What?"

"The loon is in trouble," I said. "It's on top of the ice, and black birds are attacking it. Aunt Mag isn't here. She's gone to pick up a wolf that was hit by a car."

Cedar's brain seemed to fire up then. He took the binoculars I shoved into his hands and peered out the window. "Crows," he said. "That's not good."

"We've got to do something," I said.

Cedar lowered the glasses and looked at me suspiciously. "You're not planning anything dumb, are you?"

"No!" I said. This time I knew he'd help me come up with a plan.

Cedar looked relieved. He got out of bed. "Did you call your aunt?"

I nodded. "Her mailbox is full. I can't even leave a message."

"Let's call my house," said Cedar. There was no answer there either. "Okay," he said. "I'll go over there, and while I'm doing that, you call Uncle Peter." As he was pulling on his jacket, he narrowed his eyes at me. "Don't get any nutty ideas while I'm gone, okay?"

"Okay!" I said. "Just hurry!"

He nodded and flew out the door. I found Peter's number and dialed it. It rang six times, and then his voice kicked in. "*You've reached Peter Spencer. Please leave a detailed message at the tone, and I'll return your call as soon as I'm able*." I hung up. Why was everyone gone now when I needed them? I found the number for Cedar's house and dialed.

He answered. "Hello?"

"It's me," I said. "I tried Peter but only got a message. Can your dad come?"

"There's no one here. Dad's big truck is gone. And Mom's car isn't here either. I think she might have taken Kait and Trinnie Christmas shopping in town."

"What are we going to do?"

"I'll come back over and we'll try to think of something else," Cedar said.

It made me feel better to know he was on his way. I ran to get dressed.

When Cedar got back, we tried calling everyone again. No luck. We both took another look at the loon.

"There's another crow! We've got to do something, Cedar." I felt sick thinking about the loon.

"We can't go out there, Evan. It's too dangerous."

"I know, I know," I said. "But I can't stand sitting around waiting. What if we just sit here and the loon gets pecked to death? We can't let that happen!"

Cedar's face went pale. "But you tried rescuing it before, and if Uncle Peter hadn't come, you might have fallen through the ice and drowned. We can't go out there!" He looked miserable. "We can't!"

He was right. It was too dangerous. And I had promised. But we couldn't do nothing either.

"What do you do when someone is in trouble on the ice?" I asked. "How do you rescue them if you aren't a professional rescue guy?"

Cedar frowned, thinking hard. "You could take an inflatable boat, like Uncle Peter did with you. Once your Aunt Mag used skis to go out there. Anything that spreads your weight. Sometimes Dad uses an ax and chops holes at different points to see how thick the ice is."

"Couldn't we do all those things?" I asked.

Cedar looked uncertain. "I guess," he said. "But we don't have a rescue boat. Besides, you aren't supposed to go onto the ice alone. Evan, you can't! You promised."

"I wouldn't be alone. You'd be with me," I said. Cedar shook his head so hard I thought it might fall off. "Okay!" I said. "Bad idea. What if we just get all the rescue equipment ready? How long can it take to pick up a wolf? Aunt Mag should be back soon, right?" And if she wasn't back by the time we were ready, then…I knew what I wanted to do, but I didn't want to get Cedar into trouble. Aunt Mag would just have to be back.

"So we just get everything ready?" asked Cedar, looking unconvinced.

"Exactly!" I said. "Come on. There's an old canoe in the garage and the ax is by the woodpile. I know where Aunt Mag keeps the birdseed."

"Loons don't eat birdseed," Cedar said.

"They don't?" I stared at him. "But they're birds."

Cedar snickered. "Yeah, but they're water birds. They eat fish and other junk in the lake. Have you ever seen a loon at the bird feeder?"

"Oh," I said while Cedar laughed harder. I imagined the loon trying to fit on the bird feeder perch. "I see what you mean. But the other things? We still have the box that Aunt Mag gave those hovercraft guys. Come on, Cedar."

Neither of us said anything as we raced to the garage. I pointed to the old canoe.

Cedar snorted. "Are you crazy? Do you know how much those things weigh? Even if we could lift it out of here over all this junk, it'd be too heavy to drag over the ice."

"But it would float, if we broke through," I pointed out.

"Don't be so sure," Cedar said. He stuck his finger through a hole in the bottom. "I bet this wreck has been here about a hundred years."

"Maybe it's the one from your dad's flying-canoe story," I said.

"Maybe your Auntie Mag is really the devil in disguise," Cedar said.

I laughed. "Hey, look, there's a blow-up thing, you know, like you sleep on when you're camping." I scrambled over a few gardening tools and held up a limp rubber mat.

"An air mattress," Cedar said.

"Wouldn't that work?" I asked.

"Maybe. Let's try blowing it all the way up. Hey, this might work." Cedar picked up a kickboard. "This will definitely float."

While Cedar blew up the air mattress, I found the cardboard box and the blanket in the lab. Then I ran to get the ax. We found skis under the overhang beside the house. We hauled everything down onto the beach.

Then I went in to call Aunt Mag again. Same message. I ran back to Cedar. He stood on the dock, watching the loon through the binoculars. "It's getting tired," he said. "The crows are getting bolder."

"We have to go, Cedar."

"I don't know, Evan. My dad will *totally* freak if he finds out I've been on the ice without his say-so."

"I'll tell him it was my idea."

Cedar shook his head.

"I'll tell him I forced you to do it." I was desperate.

"Yeah, that'll go over well. Makes me sound like a wimp."

"Please, Cedar. If you don't want to come, you don't have to. Just be my watcher. If anything goes wrong, you can get help."

"Evan, if you go through the ice, you'll be a giant ice cube in no time. Have you ever heard of hypothermia? And that's if you don't drown first."

"Look," I said. "I'll use the ax. How thick does the ice have to be?"

He shrugged. "A few centimeters. Ten, maybe."

I stepped off the end of the dock onto the lake and chopped a small hole in the ice. It took some work to reach the water, but there it was, black and creepy.

We both looked at it. "That's gotta be at least ten centimeters," I said.

"But it's not going to be even all the way," Cedar protested. "Evan, we have to wait!"

"If we wait, the loon will be dead and it'll be our fault!" I felt mean saying it. Cedar looked so upset. I knew I was making it hard for him. "Look, you stay here, and I'll go really slow. I won't be stupid."

"You're already being stupid," he said.

"I'm going," I said. I zipped my jacket up to the top and sat down on the dock to put on a pair of ski boots. I pretended that I wasn't scared, but I was. Cedar was right. This was a dumb idea for so many reasons. But I thought about the loon. Right now it needed our help. I had to do something. I took a deep breath and stood up.

CHAPTER 18

Broken Promise

"Okay, Evan," Cedar said, sounding panicky. "But let's think this through before we go, okay?" He plopped down and stuffed his feet into the other set of ski boots.

"You don't have to come," I said, hoping he wouldn't listen to me. He knew way more than I did about what to do if something went wrong.

"Are you kidding? I'd get in more trouble letting you go by yourself than if I come with you," he said.

I tried to get the skis to stay on my feet. No matter what I did, they kept dropping off. He looked over at what I was doing. "Have you ever used cross-country skis before?"

"Yeah, of course!" How hard could it be?

Cedar rolled his eyes and showed me how to clip my boots to the bindings. I slid forward, crossed my skis and fell down. Through his snickering, Cedar explained how to use them, "You gotta glide. It's sorta like skating, but you have to pretend you have really long blades on."

I did better after that.

"We better go apart from each another," said Cedar.

"But we only have one ax," I said.

He frowned.

"Okay, what if we tie ourselves together on a long rope?" I suggested. "That way we can be apart but be together too."

Cedar thought that was good idea and ran to search for one in the garage. While I waited, I remembered the last time I'd tried to rescue the loon and how I'd promised Aunt Mag I'd never do this again. I had really meant it. My stomach felt like it was full of rocks. She would never trust me again.

Cedar raced back with the rope. He seemed excited now that we were really going. His mood infected me, and I pushed my thoughts away. I told myself I'd make it up to Aunt Mag somehow. If nothing bad happened.

"You should go first because you're lighter," Cedar said. I nodded. I tied the rope around my waist and handed the other end to Cedar. There was no backing out now.

We put the kickboard on top of the air mattress and the box on top of that. Cedar was going to pull them behind him.

I slid away from the shore and went as far as the rope would let me out onto the lake. I bent down and chopped a hole in the ice. "We're okay here." I moved on. When I stopped again, I looked back. Cedar was peering into my last hole. I cut another one. The ice was about the same thickness. I moved forward. Cedar followed.

When we got out beyond the cove, Cedar called out to me. "You better chop more often. The ice'll be thinner. The water's deeper here."

I looked back again. We were still closer to the shore than to the loon, but not by much. I chopped a hole. The water splurted up as the ax broke through, and I nearly let go. Cedar was right, the ice *was* thinner. I went forward more slowly. The snow hissed against the bottom of my skis. *Sssss, ssss, ssss.*

The ice seemed to get thicker again, and I relaxed a little. I looked up. I could see the loon clearly now. The crows were still tormenting it, dodging and pecking while it tried to protect itself. "Hey," I shouted. "Take off!"

Two of the crows lifted into the air. The other three just hopped a few feet away. Then all five closed in again.

I waved frantically at Cedar. "Come on!" I slid forward a little faster. *Ssss, ssss, ssss. Chop, chop, chop.* It took forever. I was tempted to skip the chopping part, but I remembered that the ice near the loon had been open water yesterday.

At last I got close. The crows decided their time was up and, one after the other, they flapped into the air. The loon turned to face me, wings spread. It aimed its long bill at me, like a sword.

I stopped. "It's okay," I said softly. "We're here to help." The loon flapped and struggled to stand up. I remembered my aunt telling me why loons were clumsy on land. Masters in the water but helpless on land. Slowly I put down the ax. I heard Cedar come up and stop a little way behind me.

"Ho-lee!" he exclaimed. "That's one big, *mad* bird."

"What do we do now?" I asked. I realized that getting the loon in the box wasn't going to be easy.

"Maybe you could tackle it," suggested Cedar.

"Yeah and get punctured to death," I said. "Have you taken a look at that bill?"

"When it opens its mouth, it's a double threat," Cedar said helpfully.

"What if we put the box over it?"

"Hey," said Cedar. "Once I was with Uncle Peter and he was trying to pick up a sick fox. He put his sweater over it so it couldn't see. It stopped freaking then."

"The blanket," I said. "If we throw it over the loon, then maybe we can sneak up and get it into the box."

"Let's try it," Cedar said. He chucked the blanket to me.

I tucked it under one arm and snuck closer to the frightened bird. It spread its wings like a ginormous cape. The thing was huge! Its neck arched forward, bill ready. I stood still. A moment later, it pulled its head back again.

"Better get that blanket ready," Cedar called.

"You get the box ready," I said. I let the blanket fall open and held it in two hands. "It's okay, buddy,

I'm not going to hurt you." I spoke in a low voice. The loon shuffled uneasily and fell sideways as it tried to back away. I slid even closer. It struggled back to its feet but didn't open its wings. I figured I was close enough, and I tossed the blanket. It dropped over the loon and the weight of it held the bird down. "Quick!"

Cedar slid the box to me. I edged forward. *CRACK*. A line appeared in the new ice. I froze. I looked back at Cedar in horror.

"Don't move," he said. "I'm going to back up."

My heart thumped. I couldn't move even if I wanted to. I stood like a statue while Cedar backed away.

"I've got the rope tight now, Evan. Just reach forward and pick up the loon."

I took a deep breath. I leaned forward until I could reach the blanket. I scooped it up, loon and all. It was heavier than I expected and I sat down with a *flump*, but I didn't drop the loon. There was another *CRACK*. I forced myself to stay calm. The loon was counting on me. The ice held. I eased my bundle into the box. The loon moved but didn't struggle.

"Good going, Evan!" Cedar exclaimed.

My heart was still pounding. I stood and picked up the box in both arms. I backed up slowly a few meters.

Then I turned in a big circle. Cedar picked up the ax. He moved to the far side of the air mattress.

"Put the box on the mattress, and I'll take the kickboard," said Cedar.

I did as he said. I grabbed the cord attached to the front of the air mattress and, trying not to jerk too much, I began to ski back the way we had come. I heard Cedar gliding behind me. We were coming into the cove when Cedar said, "Oh no!"

I looked up. Lined up along the beach was a small crowd. A little way out on the ice stood Aunt Mag. Something that looked like Peter's floppy boat lay on the ground next to her feet.

"We're gonna get it," Cedar muttered.

"I don't care," I said, even though I didn't feel as brave as I sounded.

Then Cedar let out a small laugh. "You're right. I don't really either. What are they gonna do, really? We did it!"

I looked back at him. I had never seen such a big grin. I answered with my own. "Yeah! We did, didn't we?"

"Take a look, Evan," Cedar said a few minutes later. "They're all watching us through binoculars.

I wonder if this is how the loon felt for the last two weeks."

I looked up again. As Cedar said, most of the people along the shore had binoculars glued to their faces. If I hadn't known what people looked like, I might have thought they had pretty weird eyes. I noticed Aunt Mag was watching us without binoculars. I could feel her look aimed at me like a laser beam.

When we got a little closer, Cedar shouted, "We did it! We got him!"

Someone whistled; then someone else hooted; then a cheer went up. I saw people clapping and jumping up and down. Only Aunt Mag stood still and silent, watching us. I pulled the air mattress with even glides, but the closer I got to Aunt Mag, the slower I went. When we were almost there, Aunt Mag came out to meet us.

I gulped. "We were careful."

Aunt Mag didn't answer. She knelt down to the box. She placed her hands gently on the blanket. She felt the shape of the bird underneath. She lifted the corner of the cover and looked under. Then she tucked it back into the box.

"Crows attacked it," Cedar said.

She gave a single nod. Then she stood up. She looked at our equipment and at the rope attaching us to each other. My mouth felt dry but I met Aunt Mag's eye. "I tried to call you. We were afraid to wait. It was getting tired." I knew it sounded lame. I swallowed hard.

Aunt Mag nodded again. Her silence was beginning to creep me out. Cedar squinted at the shore. "How long have all those people been there?"

For the first time she spoke. "Since you were about halfway out."

Cedar and I both gaped at her.

"How long have you been here?" Cedar asked.

"Longer," came the answer.

"You didn't try to stop us," I said.

Aunt Mag shook her head. "It was your rescue. I figured my job was to rescue you, if you needed it. Peter and Mac are on their way."

"Oh, we are so going to get it," muttered Cedar.

Aunt Mag didn't say anything. She bent over and picked up the ax and the kickboard. "That loon needs attention. We need to make sure it's healthy, and then we'll have to take it someplace with open water, to let it go."

"Let it go?" I hadn't even thought about what we would do after we rescued it. "Can't we keep it?" I asked.

Aunt Mag looked at me until I felt squirmy. "You could. I'm sure it would make a fascinating pet. It seems odd to me, though, that after all this trouble you took to rescue it, you would choose to put it in another sort of captivity." She shifted the kickboard, then added, "It's up to you. It's your responsibility now."

I met Cedar's eyes and could see he was as excited about the prospect of a pet loon as I was. How many kids could say they had something like that? I looked down at the box. The blanket moved. My excitement fell away. I remembered what Aunt Mag had said. *They're wild spirits.* Somehow, I couldn't picture the loon being happy hanging out in my bedroom while I was at school all day. I knew what my choice was going to have to be.

CHAPTER 19

Wild Spirits

Cedar and I listened to the lecture by Mac and Peter.
It was pretty intense. We agreed to take an ice-safety
course from a friend of Mac's before I went home. We
had to. And we promised we'd never do anything like
this again. *Ever*. Cedar was grounded for the rest of
the holidays. It meant I'd have to hang out at his place
and we'd be doing a lot of babysitting. But it was all
worth it.

When Mac and Peter were satisfied that Cedar and
I really understood them this time, Aunt Mag hurried
me to her truck. "We have to get the loon into water as
soon as possible," she said.

I held the box on my lap and tried to keep it from
jiggling too much as we bounced along the road.

I lifted the blanket back so the loon could look out. Okay, so really it was so I could see the loon. I wanted to look at him every second. He tipped his head. Was he looking at me with those strange eyes? He sat pretty quiet.

"He must know that we aren't going to hurt him," I said.

Aunt Mag smiled. "Yes, I think he does. Being calm and quiet...well, animals know." She glanced down at the bird on my lap. "It's pretty incredible. I've never seen a loon this close up."

"Why do you think he didn't fly away at the proper time?"

"I don't suppose we'll ever get an answer to that question," she said. "The only thing I can think is that he got confused about the mild weather this fall. Global warming is affecting migration patterns."

I looked down. He turned his glossy black head, looking around. It would have been horrible if the crows had killed him. We didn't talk. Aunt Mag drove, and I looked and looked. I tried to memorize every feather. I didn't want to say goodbye to this mysterious bird. There was so much more I wanted to know.

Before I was ready, Aunt Mag turned into a parking area near a flowing river and some docks.

"Here we are," she said. She stopped the truck and shut off the engine.

The loon turned his head with short sharp movements.

"You might want to cover him up till you get him to the water so he doesn't panic," Aunt Mag said. She came around the truck to help me with the box.

Gently I pulled the corner of the blanket back over the bird's head. Aunt Mag held the box while I jumped out. Then she gave it back to me. I followed her down to the edge of the river. Slowly, I put the box on the ground next to where Aunt Mag was crouching. I felt my aunt's eyes on me.

"What do you think will happen to him?" I asked.

"I think he'll be fine," said Aunt Mag. "He'll be happy to be able to swim and dive and eat. The bird specialist said that sometimes released loons hang about for a while to eat and build their strength, but after that they usually leave."

"Migrate?" I said.

Aunt Mag nodded.

"Will he come back to your lake?"

"There aren't any guarantees but there's a pretty good chance," she said.

"Could I come back? You know, in case?" I blurted out.

Aunt Mag looked startled. "You can come back as often as you'd like, Evan." It sounded like she *wanted* me to come back.

I smiled at her. "Thanks, Aunt Mag," I said. Then I knelt down and lifted the loon, still wrapped in the blanket, out of the box. Aunt Mag waited, letting me take my time. I held the loon. He was heavy. I remembered what Aunt Mag had said about solid bones. He moved a little in my arms. I felt a hard knot in my chest.

"He can probably sense the water," said Aunt Mag softly.

I nodded. I put the bundle on the ground and lifted the blanket off the loon's head and then his back and the rest of his body. He stretched his neck forward, reaching toward the water's edge. I tilted the blanket a bit. The loon slid forward into the water. He rested there for a moment and then dove down into the cold dark murk. All he left behind were small swirls on the surface.

We stayed, watching, waiting. I tried to guess where he would come up again. Then there he was, silent and glossy and beautiful. He circled farther out but still close enough that I could see him easily.

Aunt Mag stood up. I stood beside her. Once more the loon dove and was under a long time. Once more he popped up, even farther out. He turned toward the long open water between the frozen shores and headed away from us. I didn't want him to leave. As I watched him grow smaller, a prickle started behind my eyes. I shook my head furiously. I felt Aunt Mag's hand on my shoulder, steady and strong.

"You take whatever time you need. There's no hurry."

I wanted to howl like a little kid. I kept my eyes on the loon. Then it happened. A clear wavering call, rising into the air. The loon, *my* loon, sending out his cry. I saw movement in the water. I squinted, trying to figure out what was happening. He came toward us. His wings flapped against the water, throwing up little splurts of spray on either side. I heard the *thwup, thwup, thwup* from his wings. As he got close to our little beach, he lifted off. He rose quickly, passing right over our heads.

He curved around, heading back down the river. He called once more.

The corners of Aunt Mag's mouth turned up, and she said, "I believe he's saying goodbye." She took a deep breath and let it out, now looking at me. "You have done a fine thing, Evan."

All at once I remembered Aunt Mag telling me about how when wild animals meet humans it often goes badly for the animals.

"I guess sometimes, when people and wild animals cross paths, good things can happen too," I said.

Aunt Mag looked at me for a long minute; then she looked back up to the sky. She nodded. "Yes," she said.

The lump melted in my throat. I wondered how far it was to the ocean and how long it would take to fly there.

Acknowledgments

A heartfelt thank-you to my cousins, Carolyn and Barbara Paterson, for giving me their loon story, which inspired this book, and for all their research assistance. It is my deep regret that Barbara passed away before the book was complete. Thank you also to Susan Margaret Chapman and Laurel Dee Gugler for ongoing story feedback; Jann Everard and Thereza Dos Santos for early chapter comments; Michelle Mulder for writing, editing and publishing advice; David Kennard for answering questions on ice safety and rescue; Martha and Albert Attema, whose beautiful straw-bale home inspired me to invent Mag's house.

I am extremely grateful to Harry S. Vogel, Senior Biologist and Executive Director of the Loon Preservation Committee (www.loon.org) in Moultonborough, New Hampshire, for answering my questions on loon biology and behavior. It was from Harry that I stole the term "wild spirits," which describes loons so beautifully. Any factual mistakes in the book are entirely my own. Thanks to Jill Rolph, Wildlife Biologist and Education Project Director, also of the Loon Preservation Committee, for her lecture on the Common Loon, delivered at the Harris Center for Conservation Education in Hancock, New Hampshire, and for referring me to Harry Vogel.

A special thank-you to Don Snyder, a steady light for more than twenty years, for reading the manuscript, offering astute suggestions and for so much more; to Harris and Emmett Snyder, who keep me laughing, and for cooking some meals so I didn't have to; and to Sarah Harvey for her editorial skill and guidance, her sense of humor and for saying yes to the manuscript.

To all of you, thank you, thank you.

When Rebecca Upjohn was growing up, she spent her summers listening to loons, and she has never lost the thrill of hearing their calls. She has worked herding sheep, photographing buildings, selling books and producing a short film. She and her husband live with their two teenage sons and a dog in Toronto. Rebecca's first book, *Lily and the Paper Man* (Second Story Press), was published in 2007. To learn more about Rebecca, visit her website: www.rebeccaupjohn.com.

ORCA
YOUNG
READER

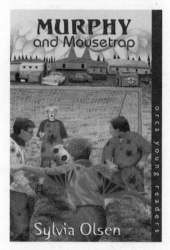

978-1-55143-344-8 $7.95 pb

Murphy's mother has just moved Murphy and their cat Mousetrap back to the reserve. Although he belongs to the First Nation, Murphy is sure that he won't fit in, and he worries about Mousetrap, who has always been an indoor cat. When a bunch of local boys drag him to their soccer practice, put him in goal and pelt him with balls, he believes that his worst fear has come true. But he seems to be discovering a new talent at the same time. And perhaps he has misjudged. Being a light-skinned city boy thrust onto a reserve far from the city is not easy, but maybe Murphy has what it takes.

ORCA
YOUNG
READER

978-1-55469-169-2 $7.95 pb

It's no secret. Never before has the Long Inlet
Tribal School produced so many talented soccer players.
In this sequel to *Murphy and Mousetrap*, the Formidable
Four—Murphy, Danny, Jeff and Albert—are moving up
to middle school and trying out for the soccer team. They're
pretty confident that they will all make the team, but once
the tryouts begin, Albert, the tribal-school superstar, plays
like a second stringer and acts like a jerk. When Murphy
and his friends discover the truth about their teammate,
they realize that Albert is playing a whole different game.

ORCA
YOUNG
READER

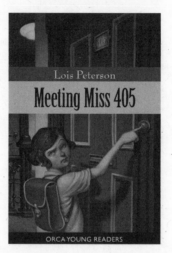

978-1-55469-015-2 $7.95 pb

Life is hard enough for Tansy with her mom away indefinitely and her dad making a mess of things at home. Then her dad sends her down the hall to a wrinkly old babysitter named Miss Stella, who doesn't even own a TV. Or a computer. Or a car. She eats brown spaghetti and Bird's custard. What kind of a babysitter is she?